Girls on Tour

Lulu White

Girls on Tour by Lulu White

Cover by Jennifer Kirkham

ISBN: 9798352723081

1

"I've never seen a penis that big. Honestly this thing was like the size of my arm!" Lauren smirked, pouring herself a large glass of wine.

"Oh please!" The others exclaimed, laughing their heads off.

"No. Stop this is making me feel a bit sick. I mean who actually wants one that big? Isn't a vagina like five inches long anyway? So anymore than that is a waste right?" Said Juliette.

"It's not five inches! It can take more than that. Well at least mine can." Lauren burst out laughing. "Right ladies drink up, reservation's at nine and I don't want to be the only one drunk."

Lauren, Juliette, Nancy and Ria had been best friends since secondary school. They'd met as 12 year olds and

15 years later they were still as thick as thieves. Since they were 18, they'd always done an annual trip somewhere. This year they'd chosen Barcelona for five nights of sun, sea and sex.

"Ok *vamos chicas!*" Squealed Lauren as they each knocked back a shot of tequila, grabbed their bags and headed out of their airbnb. Their apartment was located in *Eixample*, Nancy had managed to get a great deal on a four bed apartment on the fourth floor of a gorgeous modernista building complete with terrace and balconies off each room.

"Nance I've got to say you've excelled yourself this time. Bit of an improvement on the shit hole Ria found us in Paris last year." Lauren mocked. Ria rolled her eyes as the girls reminisced about the weird 'host' and the lack of beds which had meant two of the girls sharing a blow up bed on a mezzanine floor with hardly any head room.

"I liked the apartment babe." Juliette smiled at Ria.

"Oh piss off all of you, it was the best I could find in *Le Marais* for our shitty budget."

They'd never been to Barcelona before and the first thing that struck them compared to London was how wide the streets were and how spacious and open it felt. As they walked through *Eixample* towards *Plaza Catalunya* they could hear the music and laughter from roof terraces and balconies. Whereas in London the night was usually over by eleven when the bars closed, one, two latest if you went to a club, in Barcelona people didn't even think about leaving the house until at least nine, usually later. And if you wanted to go to a club, don't even think about turning up before midnight.

"So I think we just carry straight on down the *Rambla* and then turn left into the gothic. We're looking for *Carrer Ample*." Nancy instructed, reading directions from her phone.

"Nancy?" Nancy looked up and was startled to see her old friend from Uni, Pablo.

"Hey Nancy! What are you doing here?"

"Oh my god Pablo! Guys this is Pablo. We were at Uni together. Pablo, this is Lauren, Juliette and Ria. We've literally just got here, it's our first night."

"*Encantada chicas*. Wow Nancy you didn't tell me you had such hot friends. Where you girls heading tonight? I'm just on my way to meet my cousin Samuel. You want to join us?" Lauren was already sizing up Pablo. Tall, dark, handsome with a bit of an edge. A small nose ring, flesh hole in his left ear, low riding jeans with his treasure trail just peeking out below his t-shirt. He looked like a skater boy, which usually wasn't her thing. But she liked his confidence.

"We've got a dinner reservation but maybe we could meet you guys after?" Said Juliette.

"Fuck the reservation, let's go get drunk." Lauren said, linking her arm through Pablo's.

If someone had asked the girls to explain where the bar was, none of them would have been able to remember. Pablo took them through a maze of alleyways before they ended up at a shop front that looked closed. He knocked on the door and a man came out to lead them in. Through the shop they went before it opened into a shot bar with thumping music and low lights.

"What is this place?" Nancy said, taking full ownership of the fact it was her friend that had taken them here. Ria and Juliette were too busy posing in front of the foliage wall, where a neon sign read '*Destination Unknown*'.

"That's a pretty shit name for a bar." Lauren said to Pablo as they grabbed a booth.

"You're a feisty one mami" Pablo said, holding eye contact as he placed his hand on her inner thigh.

"You like that do you?" She teased.

"Do you like it?" He teased back, edging his fingers up to her knickers. Lauren felt herself get wet.

"You wouldn't dare." She teased. "Not with all these people about?"

"Do you want me to?" He asked eagerly, taken aback he'd only just met this girl but she was game. Without saying a word, Lauren opened her thighs beneath the table and placed his hand on her crotch so he could feel the wetness seeping through her knickers.

"You know how much I want to taste that right now?" He poked the tip of his finger underneath her knickers and slipped it inside her. Just enough to feel her warm wet pussy. Then as quick as he'd entered, he took his hand out and swigged from his bottle of estrella.

"That's not fair." Lauren cooed, stroking his thigh and noticing his bulging package. Without saying anything, Pablo took Lauren by the hand and through the bar to a back room. He closed the door and knelt down, peeling down her knickers and kissing her inner thigh before working his way onto her clit. She moaned in ecstasy, arching her back and holding onto the shelves behind her. He worked away, licking and caressing her cunt as she held his head down, moaning until she was about to climax. Then he stood up and unzipped his jeans. Swivelling her round, he entered her with his eight inch member. He gripped her hair with one hand and held her ass cheek with the other. He fucked her hard before he filled her up with cum, unable to contain it any longer.

"Where's Lauren and Pablo?" Juliette said, bringing six shots of tequila to the table.

"God knows." Ria said, hitting back the shot.

"So Samuel, do you live here?" Asked Juliette.

"Ya, I live in *Gràcia*, you know it?"

"No is that in the city?"

"Yes but it's a bit further out. I like it there. Less touristy. But here is fun for the weekend. I get to meet girls like you." He said smiling.

"Hey Samu!" A gorgeous Spanish looking girl came rushing over, kissing him on both cheeks. They chatted in Spanish before Samuel introduced her.

"Hey girls, this is Nina. She's an old friend. Her brother runs this bar."

"Wow, three gorgeous ladies. I don't know how you do it Samu. You're not that good looking!" Nina laughed, kissing each of the girls on the cheek. When she got to Juliette she stopped and held her hands.

"You're beautiful chica. Those eyes. Wow. Can I buy you a drink?"

Juliette blushed, "Oh thank you but…" She trailed off as Nina rushed to the bar, returning with two cocktails.

"I hope you like margaritas. They're my favourite." She smiled, holding eye contact.

"Ok I think Nina might have the hots for you Jools." Nancy laughed, reapplying her lipstick in the bathroom mirror.

"What do you think? You ready to come to the dark side?" Ria said.

"Hello ladies!" In marched Lauren, looking triumphant.

"Where have you been?" Juliette asked, thankful for the interruption.

"Getting the best sex of my life in the store cupboard." She declared, rearranging her dress and reapplying her lipstick. The girls exchanged glances. "What have I missed?"

"Not a lot, but Samu's just picked up so here's your nose bag." Nancy tossed a bag of white powder to Lauren who immediately dabbed her pinky finger and rubbed it onto her gums.

"Nice. Anyone got a note?"

Ria passed Lauren a note and they headed into the cubicle. Nancy took a key and sniffed whilst Juliette looked on.

"Sure we can't tempt you?" She asked Juliette.

"You know what. Yeah. I will have some."

"Guys? Guys? Are you hearing this. Juliette's getting in on the action!"

"Yes Jools!" Hooted Lauren.

A few lines later and it was suddenly midnight. And the night was only just beginning.

2

"Hey girls, you wanna go dancing?" Nina shouted over the music, wiping her nose as she took a long line.

Lauren and Pablo were practically having sex in the booth. The coke had made them both extra horny. Suddenly Lauren grabbed Nina and started to kiss her.

"Hey, hey, sexy lady. I've only got eyes for one chica here." Nina winked at Juliette and went to the bar to get more drinks whilst the others discussed where to head to next.

"I know this great club that's like a fairground. It's called *La Fira*. It's got clowns and fair rides and shit. Seriously we gotta go." Samu said, clapping his hands for everyone to move.

Nancy was seriously considering fucking Samuel. Like Pablo, he wasn't really her type. But something about the

Barcelona air was making her really dig this guy. Or maybe it was the coke. Who cares. She was 27 years old, single, with a 23 inch waist, a red mane like Jessica Rabbit and a first in History from Cambridge under her belt. Ok she hadn't done too much with her degree work wise since she'd left but she had experiences. She'd travelled. She'd lived. And Samuel would be just another experience.

"Let's go." Nancy said. And just like that, they stumbled out *Destination Unknown* for *La Fira*.

The queue was long. And the coke was starting to wear off.

"Let's just go back to the airbnb. It's like 3am and we're still not in." Ria was getting impatient.

"You feeling left out because you're not with anyone?" Nina pouted.

"You're not with Juliette babe. She's not gay so you're wasting your time."

"You're just jealous because I didn't come onto you."

"You're not my type."

"Oh and what is your type if it's not smoking hot?" Nina cackled.

"Let's just say I like my women a bit less arrogant." Ria retorted.

"Babe don't let her wind you up." Lauren said stroking Ria's arm.

"Guys we're next." Juliette said. And they piled in the door.

Acrobats hung from the ceiling. There were clowns on penny farthings giving out shots. In the centre beautiful women strutted down the catwalk in nothing but body paint.

"Bottoms up!" Pablo said, holding out the palm of his hand with 7 white tablets on. Juliette could feel the music in her veins. Like literally running through her veins. Her whole body was vibrating and Nina's body seemed to be moving to the same beat. She clasped Nina's hand and put it on her abdomen, moving it up and down her torso.

"I'm not just for fun you know." Nina shouted over the music. "Don't just be teasing me because you're high." Juliette put her finger to Nina's mouth to silence her before leaning in. Her whole body felt alive. So this is what it feels like to kiss a girl. Nina was passionate. Her tongue almost turgid. They danced for what seemed like hours. Dancing and kissing like teenagers. Oblivious to anyone around them. Juliette felt giddy.

"Come on let's go." Ria stormed over, grabbing Juliette by the arm.

"I would say this is a cock block. But I don't have a cock." Nina chuckled. "See you tomorrow mi amor." Juliette gave a shy smile. And then they were gone.

3

Back at the airbnb Ria was furious.

"What's up with you?" Juliette asked, eating a bag of ham flavoured crisps, covering herself in crumbs. Her eyes wild with smudged mascara as the drugs started to wear off.

"You're not gay Juliette. So why are you snogging the face off Nina?"

"I dunno, I just got carried away I guess."

"But you liked it?" Ria asked.

"Well yeah…yeah I did. I mean nothing's going to actually happen Ria. It's just a bit of fun." Ria scoffed.

"I'm going to bed. Night." And she slammed her bedroom door.

Meanwhile at *La Fira*, Nancy was really trying her hardest to flirt with Samuel. But he didn't seem interested at all. She felt like a fool. He was too busy dancing and drinking to seem to even notice her and Lauren and Pablo had disappeared again.

Pablo had snuck Lauren into the boys toilets. They'd locked themselves in the end cubicle and she was on her knees begging for his cock. He held his member, slapping her cheek lightly which she went wild for. She put her hands down her pants and began to rub her clit as she licked her lips. He entered her mouth and rested his head on the back of the door. She began sucking his cock whilst simultaneously teasing her clit. She'd done this before. Just as he was about to come there was a bang on the door. Someone shouting in Spanish. Pablo quickly zipped up his jeans and Lauren rearranged herself.

"We better go. This guy is pissed. Seriously."
They rushed out giggling onto the dancefloor which had begun to get pretty empty. It was 5.30am. Lauren grabbed Nancy and they headed back to the airbnb. Promising to meet up with the boys and Nina again at the beach later that day.

4

It was midday and Lauren finally woke up to join the others nursing sore heads in the lounge.

"So I'm thinking we go here tonight." Ria said, showing the girls a picture of a castle.

"We're not on a school trip Ria. We're going out tonight. You'll be fine after a couple of drinks."

"It's a club Lauren. It's called *El Bitch*. It's a gay club in a castle on the top of *Montjuic* Mountain. It's not fair you guys getting all the action. It's my holiday too."

"Juliette didn't seem to need a gay club to get lucky last night." Nancy teased.

"Guys don't." Juliette was starting to feel a bit weird about last night. She wasn't gay. So why did she come onto Nina? Why did she feel so good kissing her? Why did she fall asleep thinking about her and them together in bed? She'd always appreciated the female form. When she watched porn, she watched the women. Their perfectly formed breasts, their curves, their soft skin. Could she be bi? Or had she just been with men previously because that was the norm? Maybe she didn't even like men? No, she definitely liked men, but she'd never felt like she had last night with any guy recently. Not since school really.

"Yeah maybe we could invite Nina tonight." Lauren joked. But Juliette wanted Nina to come, in more ways than one.

Nancy wasn't feeling too hungover. Unlike the others she was pretty strict when it came to her health. She always took rehydration salts before and after drinking, as well as activated charcoal to draw out the toxins. But above all she believed strongly in plenty of fresh fruit, vegetables and exercise to get her out of any hungover slump.

"Guys I'm going to go for a wander, get a juice and head to this yoga class. Can I tempt anyone to join me?" She looked at Juliette, she was usually her best bet when it came to exercise on holiday.

"Do not look at me Nance. I ate an entire family bag of ham flavoured crisps before bed. That's how drunk I was." She laughed.

"I literally cannot think of anything worse Nancy. You're on your own there pal." Lauren added.

"Babe I'd love to but I'd actually be concerned about having a heart attack after the amount of coke I had last night." Ria said, holding her head in her hands.

"Sod the lot of you!" Nancy laughed. "I'll meet you at the beach for midday?"

"Yep see you there." They called as she shut the door.

Freedom. There was something liberating about being in a foreign country, left to your own devices. Nancy had travelled extensively with friends but also alone, and it was the latter she enjoyed the most. Total freedom to do exactly as she wanted. Dressed in ribbed yoga shorts and a boxy crop top, Nancy's perfectly toned stomach was on show. In London she always covered up the body she worked so hard on, but here in Barcelona everyone seemed to celebrate their bodies so why shouldn't she. She passed a smoothie stand on *La Rambla* and ordered their *detox* one. Following instructions on her phone she took a left and found herself in a small plaza where she looked for a sign to *Shakti Move*. She'd been following the yoga studio on instagram and had it earmarked for this trip. It was badly sign posted but she managed to find an unassuming entrance next to a cocktail bar of all places. Three flights of stairs later she entered a small dark internal room that stank of incense. A skinny bearded man with googly eyes slowly put down his vintage paperback of *The Art of Tantra* and gazed up as if he wasn't really there at all.

"Hi, sorry, do you speak English?" Nancy asked.

"Of course." Came the reply. "It is only the English who do not speak other languages." He smiled curtly.

"Yeah, sorry." Nancy stumbled embarrassed. Since when did staff treat customers so rudely she thought to herself. "I just wondered if I could join the next class? I was passing by so just thought I'd check if you had space." She asked nervously. Why was she nervous? She was the one wanting to pay for a class for christ sake.

"It's starting now." He waved her through to a door. "Pay after." And with that he reopened his book.

Nancy tried to creep into the class incognito. She'd specifically checked the timetable that morning but the class was well into a flow, so she was sure it hadn't just started and now she felt rude. That guy was a dick she decided. A stupid wanky dick.

"*Endereza tu pierna. Tu pierna! Si.*"

Nancy wasn't sure what the man had just told her to do but it appeared she had done it. Better concentrate, she thought. As she bent down into child's pose she felt strangely exposed. *God I hope these shorts haven't gone see through. My bums about to burst out of here!*

"*Inglesa?*" The teacher asked, and when Nancy didn't reply, "English?"

"Yes yes I'm English" Nancy replied navigating a tricky side plank. He propped up her hip and lengthened her arm. His dark green eyes lingered just a second too long on Nancy's.

"The English are always late. Always in such a hurry. In my class...time to slow down." He winked at the other students and carried on with the flow. *How bloody patronising.*

By the end of the sequence Nancy was in a hurry to get back. Perhaps a yoga class hadn't been the best idea after a big night. The room was hot and sweaty with bodies and the sun was strong against the window panes. She needed water and fast. But she was forced to remain seated for ten more excruciating minutes as the teacher, Juan Felipe, practised a chant of oms as he intermittently hit brass gongs. The ringing of which was enough to make Nancy feel violently sick. Finally as the class shuffled out bidding their namastes, Nancy made her exit. Grappling with her euros to pay wanky dick face on her way out. But as she reached the exit, she felt a hand on her shoulder.

"Don't tell me." Juan Felipe closed his eyes in mock thought. "You're hungover." He smiled revealing a gold tooth which for some bizarre reason just worked. He was a typical hipster bohemian, long hair tied into a top knot and a shark tooth necklace choking his neck. If he hadn't reminded Nancy of James Franco she would have found him too try hard and spiritual for her liking.

"Yeah sorry, I probably shouldn't have come. I was just passing and I follow your studio on instagram. I've done a couple of your youtube videos." She explained. Why was she explaining herself. She really must be hungover. This nervousness was seriously unlike the usually assertive Nancy.

"Next time. Come without those.." He waved his hands in the hair as if conjuring up the word. "Toxins." He smiled. "See you around..." He gestured for her name.

"Nancy." She replied.

"See you around Miss Nancy."

5

Barcelona beach was heaving. There were roller bladers, street dancers, people selling everything from massages to *cervezas* to hash. Apparently One Direction were staying in the W hotel, which accounted for the additional groups of females swarming around the far end of the beach hoping to catch a glimpse of them. The girls had walked from their apartment. Hungover in 30 degree heat. As promised Nancy was there waiting for them. She'd already been in the sea to cool off post yoga, and was now horizontal with her shades on going over the awkwardness of her interaction with Juan Felipe.

Ria returned from the 7/11 with four cans of kopparberg fruit ciders.

"This should sort you all out."

They sipped the sugary goodness as they scanned somewhere to lay their towels. They'd received no communication from Pablo, Samuel or Nina but they knew that was the Spanish way so they were pretty sure they'd turn up at some point.

"Hey girls. You look like you like to party? Am I right?" An impossibly tall blonde Dutch guy bent down to chat with a handful of flyers. "I'm Pieter, mind if I join you?"

"Actually Pieter, let me save you some time here. We don't want to go to an expensive pool party with a load of teenagers. But thanks for your time." Ria rolled over and put her sunglasses down.

"Ria!" Lauren exclaimed. "Fucking hell rude. Sorry Pieter, she's not our spokesperson. Please join us."
Pieter laughed awkwardly.

"It's ok it's ok. I am here to sell tickets, but I sell other stuff you might be interested in too..."
At this, Ria removed her sunglasses and rolled back onto her stomach to face him.

"Perhaps I was a little hasty. What have you got?"

By the time Pablo and Samuel arrived, the girls had procured their treats for the evening.

"Where's Nina?" Juliette asked. Kicking herself for looking so needy. No hello, just where's Nina. God she could be a real idiot sometimes. No wonder she was still single.

"Ah I hate to disappoint but she's busy. She's a busy lady you know." Pablo put his hand to his chest in mock apology.

"But she's coming to *El Bitch* tonight. If that's still the plan?" Samuel asked.

"Yes it is the plan." Ria confirmed before anyone could suggest otherwise.

"Will you still come?" Lauren purred.

"I think we can make an exception on this occasion." Pablo looked at Samuel who nodded as he drank his beer.

"To be honest with you, it is a good night there. I've been before with friends and it's really something. The views you know." He made a circle with his thumb and forefinger to signal OK.

"Great so we'll meet you there? Unless you fancy some pre drinks at ours before?" Lauren suggested.

"Drinks sound good. Text me the address." Pablo said, rolling on top of Lauren and pushing his body against hers as they made out in the sand.

"Seriously?" Ria threw her hands up and rolled onto her front.

6

Back at the apartment the girls got ready for their night
out. They'd bought some *sangria* from the supermarket
and had *El Taxi* booming out the speakers as they did
their makeup. Ria was taking far longer to get ready than
usual. She opted for a dark maroon lipstick and a silver
slip dress. She'd styled her dreadlocks into a high bun on
her head to expose her razor sharp check bones.
Everyone always remarked on how similar she looked to
Zoë Kravitz. She was always striking even though she
never wore makeup, so when she did dress up she looked
like a film star.

Lauren was wearing hot pants and a crop top to expose
her belly piercing. She was all blonde hair and blue eyes,
not a natural beauty compared to the other three but she
definitely had sex appeal! Her boobs were pretty perfect

too. Big but pert, Juliette always told her if she ever had a boob job she'd be showing the surgeon her rack.

Nancy opted for a co-ord of high waisted palazzo trousers in a bold print with a matching crop top. Her big bouncy red curls resting on her shoulders.

"I can't explain how awkward that yoga class was this morning. I can confirm I won't be going back tomorrow." She said, joint in one hand, *sangria* in the other.

"I think you wanted to fuck him." Lauren declared.

"Mate, he had a gold tooth." Nancy cried to which even Ria couldn't help but laugh. She put her arm around Nancy.

"You and I aren't having much luck this trip are we."

"Guys, it's been one night! Chill out. There are plenty more opportunities to get jiggy." Lauren reassured them.

"When are the guys coming?" Juliette asked. She purposefully didn't mention Nina. She had butterflies at the thought she might be coming too. Surely she'd be at *El Bitch* even if she didn't come for pre drinks. It was 9pm and Pablo had said they'd be there half an hour ago.

At quarter past, the door buzzed and up came Pablo, Samuel and Nina holding a crate of beers, a bottle of tequila and a bag of coke. Juliette busied herself in the kitchen fetching glasses. Nina followed her, and pushed her up against the fridge.

"Aren't you going to say hello?" She asked, kissing her slowly. Juliette's heart was racing. She did not want the girls to see this. Last night was weird enough but at least they were all too drunk to remember the details, she hoped.

"Not here." Juliette whispered. Nina held her hands up in mock protest.

"Get your coke kids!" Shouted Lauren. That's what Juliette needed. Some confidence. She marched through, grabbed the note and snorted a fat line. It stung, and she dabbed her nostril to make sure there wasn't any blood. Lauren was rubbing the residue onto her gums and Nancy and Ria were chatting to Samuel and Pablo on the terrace, sharing a joint. It must have been eleven by the time they left the apartment. You didn't need a taxi to *El Bitch*. There was a bus that collected you from one of the nearby gay bars. They piled on, promising the Drag Queen who stamped them on they were all gay. For a moment Ria thought Lauren was going to give the game away, but Pablo played the part well, holding hands with Samuel.

7

Nina arrived at *El Bitch* like some sort of celebrity. Everyone seemed to know her, or know of her, and she couldn't walk a few steps without someone coming over to chat or offer to buy her a drink. She looked like a supermodel. She was 5,8 with slicked back bronde hair down to her shoulders. She was wearing a chocolate leather corset and matching high waisted trousers with platform heels. Her arms had tiny tattoos dotted around, so dainty you may miss them. But they were there. A pair of abstract boobs on her inner bicep, a line drawing of a dandelion, a trail of red ants and berber symbols only she knew the meaning of. Her lips were full, her eyes an intense green brown. A gold bar piercing at the nape, Juliette wondered what other piercings and tattoos Nina might have. She'd often toyed with the idea of a nipple piercing but she'd been too squeamish and never gone through with it. Nina was who she wanted to be. In another life.

Juliette went to the bar to get a drink. Nina was busy chatting with everyone else but her. Had she given her the cold shoulder in the kitchen? Ria was in her element on the dancefloor, Lauren was somewhere with Pablo and Nancy had got chatting to one of the only straight guys in the venue who was there with his brother. Suddenly it dawned on Juliette. She was boring. Beautiful but boring. Half French, half Irish, Juliette was a petite 5, 3". Small but perfectly formed. With marble white skin, green eyes and a mane of shiny brunette hair. She always turned heads. And yet she was always single.

"You ok? You look like you're having a moment." It was Nina. She was back. Juliette couldn't help but beam.

"What do you want to drink?" She asked.

"I'll get something in a bit." Nina said, looking intently at Juliette. "I want to remember tonight. Let's go." Nina said and took Juliette by the hand. They went out a side door by the stage out into the warm Spanish air. They were alone with the sound of the *cicadas*. Juliette followed Nina up the metal fire escape onto the roof of the castle. The sky looked like it was full of a thousand fireflies. Juliette found herself straddling Nina, grinding her pelvis into her, kissing her neck and unzipping her corset to release her buxom breasts. She toyed with Nina's nipples. Licking each one, burying her head into her boobs, smelling her perfume and feeling her soft skin with her lips and hands. Unsure what to do next, Nina took her queue and began to kiss Juliette's neck and shoulders. Suddenly she lay down and pulled Juliette towards her so she was sat on her face. Nina breathed heavily through Juliette's pants. She was only wearing some lace knickers beneath her LBD so it was easy for Nina to access her sweet warm pussy. She licked slowly through the pants, driving Juliette wild. She could have come just like that but she didn't want it to stop. Nina pulled her pants to one side, desperate to finally taste her prize. Her face was sodden with the juices and she lapped them up like she was starving. Juliette moved her body rhythmically. She listened to her body. This felt good. Better than good. Suddenly she exploded, coming on Nina's tongue, moaning and panting. Nina kissed her and Juliette was surprisingly turned on by the taste of herself. She tried to take Nina's trousers down but she stopped her.

"Let's get back to the party. Plenty of time for that later."

Samuel was definitely not into Nancy. And Lauren was starting to get the impression that maybe he was into her instead. When he danced with her, his hands lingered a little bit too long on her waist. When she was with Pablo she saw him watching. So when Lauren found herself in the toilet with Pablo and Samuel doing lines, she wasn't surprised when Samuel came onto her, even if it was in front of Pablo.

"Dam Lauren. That ass. Seriously."
Pablo laughed as he rolled a joint to smoke outside.

"If I hadn't already fucked your friend, you might be in with a chance Samu. I may be horny but I am faithful to my holiday romances."

"It wouldn't be the first time me and Pablo have shared a girl you know."

"Is this guy for real." Lauren laughed, bending down to take another line.

Pablo came up behind her and stroked her ass.

"You ever been with two guys?" He asked, putting the joint behind his ear.

"God no. None of the men I've been with would want to share me….but I could be tempted." She grabbed Samuel by the collar and kissed him lightly whilst Pablo kissed her neck.

"How do you want it my Queen." Samuel asked, as he knelt down. Lauren hitched her skirt up and grabbed his head of curls. Thrusting it onto her pussy.

"Now lick." She ordered. God what was coming over her. She had two guys at her disposal and it felt good.

Pablo was kissing her neck from behind, watching as his boner grew harder and harder. He found it a real turn on to watch his girl get pleasure from someone else. Lauren reached behind for his cock. She wanted to feel it hard against her back and ass.

"I want you to fuck me in the ass." She told him. Pablo sat down on the toilet seat waiting for Lauren to sit on him. She eased herself on to his sizable cock, moaning. Samuel watched awaiting instructions.

"Now fuck me Samu." He bent down to get the right angle and entered Lauren with his thick black cock. Both boys were pumping away, Lauren was in ecstasy. She'd done it herself at home with two dildos before, but this was the real thing and she loved it. Samuel went first. He pulled out as he was coming, covering Lauren's pussy. She loved the sight of her pussy covered in cum. Pablo went next, filling up Lauren's ass. Filled with cum, Lauren was still desperate to climax. She pushed Samuel's head down.

"Lick it up." She ordered. And he obliged. With Pablo's cock still deep inside her ass, and Samuel licking her pussy whilst fingering her at the same time, Lauren finally came. Exhausted, the trio collapsed on a heap of the toilet floor. They freshened up, exchanged a kiss, had a quick line and headed outside for a post-coital joint.

8

Nancy's straight guy was a non-starter. He said he was straight but Nancy was starting to get the impression that he might actually just be in the closet. He certainly seemed very interested in the live sex show that was happening on the stage and when they asked for a volunteer to join the two stacked guys that needed oiling up, he didn't exactly resist when his brother pushed him forward. Ria meanwhile was trying to chat up a Spanish girl without actually speaking any Spanish.

"You have amazing eyes." She shouted over the music.

"*Qué?*"

"You have amazing eyes. Your eyes. I love your eyes." She said, pointing to her eyes.

"Thank you. You also have good eyes." The girl replied awkwardly.

"What's your name?"

"Elena. And you?"

"I'm Ria."

It was going nowhere. She was in one of the best gay cities in the world but without any Spanish she was struggling to turn on her usual charm. How did Juliette manage to find the only English speaking hot lesbian without even going to a gay club. Where even was Juliette and Nina.

"Hey I'm ready for round two." Juliette said, squeezing Nina's hand as she chatted to yet more people she knew.

"Hey guys this is my friend Juliette."

"Hi," Juliette said awkwardly. She didn't want to make friends. She wanted to fuck Nina. But now that Nina had had her way with her, she didn't seem as interested. Had she done something wrong? She'd never been with a woman before. Maybe she'd not been very good. Can you even be not very good at receiving?

"You ok baby?" Nina asked, sensing something was troubling Juliette.

"I said I'm ready for round two. Let's get out of here. We can go back to our apartment." Juliette suggested.

"It's only 3am Juliette. The night is young baby. You want some coke? You flagging?" Nina passed Juliette a wrap and turned her back on her, carrying on her conversation. How had this happened? How was Juliette the one chasing after Nina now? Feeling embarrassed and pissed off, Juliette headed to the toilet. She looked at herself in the mirror. Took a fat line, dabbed her nose and reapplied her lipstick.

"Hey you got a hairbrush?" Juliette asked one of the dancers who'd just come in.

"I don't speak English sorry." She tutted.

Juliette wanted to go. *What was that woman's problem?* No wonder they called it *El Bitch*. Without saying a word to Nina she found Ria, Lauren and Nancy having a joint outside and told them she wanted to go.

"Oh my god. You got blown out by Nina." Lauren slapped her thighs.

"I did not get blown out by Nina. I'm just tired and I want to go. So you guys stay if you want but I need the key ok." Juliette said, visibly pissed off.

"I'll come back with you." Ria said. "I'm knackered anyway and I've had an absolute fail on the chat up front."

So Ria and Juliette took one of the taxis waiting outside the venue and headed back to the apartment.

"You ok Jools?" Ria asked, holding her hand.

"I did stuff with Nina…and I liked it. And I'm not sure what that means but all I know is that now she's not interested in me and I feel like an idiot."

"You're not an idiot." Ria said. "Look at me. You're not an idiot. Nina is a beautiful woman who came on to you. You reciprocated and it's her fucking loss man if she's not into you. I knew she was fucking weird from the start. Way too arrogant…" Juliette leant in and kissed Ria.

"What are you doing?" Ria asked.

"Am I a shit kisser? Is that what it is? Nina's the only girl I've ever kissed. Maybe she knows that. She knows I'm inexperienced."

"You kiss fine." Ria said, leaning in again. The kiss felt natural. Ria pulled away, unsure whether she was still helping her or whether they were kissing because they both liked it.

"Why are you pulling away then?" Juliette said, unclicking her seatbelt and straddling Ria. Ria couldn't believe what was happening. She liked Juliette but she'd always suppressed her feelings because she wasn't into women and hey, she didn't want to ruin their friendship. But now Juliette was coming onto her. She pushed her back gently.

"Jools…we shouldn't do this. I don't want to ruin our friendship."

"We're on holiday Ria. The rules are different here. The others won't be back for hours. I want you to be the first woman I sleep with properly."

The cab pulled up at the apartment and Ria and Juliette jumped out. Juliette loved Ria's style. Her mother was from Ghana and she made a point of buying from up and coming West African clothing designers. Her fingers were covered in chunky gold rings and her cheekbones were the envy of everyone. It happened so naturally. They tumbled into bed, stripping down to their underwear. Ria was wearing emerald green lace knickers, she had a toned athletes figure with a rippling six pack but her boobs were bigger than Juliette imagined. Hidden under baggy tops were two perfectly pert rounded mounds. She put her mouth to the nipple and worked her way down Ria's body. Ria let her peel down her pants, as she spread her legs and got the best head of her life. Why was sex always better when it was taboo? Ria pulled Juliette on top of her and flipped her over so she was on the bottom. She started to thumb Juliette's clit. Small circular motions before she bowed her head to taste her. Her pussy tasted of strawberries it was so sweet. She laid on top of Juliette, grinding her clit onto hers. Two wet pussies rubbing up against one another. The girls writhed and moaned before Ria opened her legs and slotted Juliette between her so they were scissoring. Ria reached into her side drawer and pulled out a double ended dildo.

"I always come prepared." She smiled, inserting one end into her pussy and the other into Juliette's. They fucked like this as they rubbed their clits against one another. Juliette came first, followed by Ria. Then they lay wrapped in each others arms. And it felt like the most natural thing in the world.

Juliette's phone started to vibrate. It was Nina. Oblivious, Ria was rolling a joint to smoke on the balcony. Juliette wanted to answer but she let it ring off. Sex with Ria was amazing but she still couldn't help but wonder what it would be like with Nina too.

9

The next morning, Ria and Juliette were woken up to Lauren and Nancy giggling as they came through the door.

"Honey, we're home." Lauren called.

It was 9am. Ria came out in her bed shirt.

"You guys are gonna feel like shit today." She said. Putting the kettle on to make some coffee.

"And you look like you've had a good seeing to. Did you get lucky in the end?" Nancy teased.

Ria couldn't hide the smile from her face.

"Nope just a good night's sleep ladies."

Juliette came out of her bedroom. She felt like Lauren and Nancy must know what had happened between her and Ria last night. She was trying to act normal but the more she tried the more un normal she felt.

"Coffee?" Ria asked Juliette.

"Yes please." Lauren answered.

"Yeah coffee would be great thanks." Juliette said politely.

"None for me thanks. I'm gonna try and get a couple of hours kip before the beach." Nancy said, skulking off into the bedroom.

"So I've already filled Nancy in. But I totally fucked Pablo and Samu last night. At the same time." Lauren declared, falling onto the couch.

The girls practically spat their coffee out.

"What the fuck Lauren? You let those assholes take advantage of you like that?" Ria was furious.

"No Ria. They worked for me. I wore the trousers and it felt fucking good. I had them both eating out the palm of my hand. Or should I say my pussy."

"Jesus Lauren." Juliette got up and walked to the bathroom. "I'm going for a shower."

"What happened to feminism bitches? What happened to sexual liberation. Doing what feels good. Fuck society. Seriously. I did me last night and it felt fucking awesome. Can you pair say the same?"

Juliette pretended she didn't hear this last bit and locked herself in the shower. Ria had the feeling Juliette might be regretting last night.

By lunch time, the girls had finally dressed and were pretty starving. They headed to an all day brunch place that Pablo had recommended called *Milk*. They ordered *huevos rancheros* and *bloody marías* and planned the rest of their day.

"So I'm pretty whacked. I'm thinking we chill at the beach, then an early dinner out, a couple of drinks and home before midnight. We don't want to burn ourselves out." Nancy suggested.

"Sounds good to me." Said Juliette, opening a message from Nina:

What you doing today? Wanna sneak over to mine for some fun?

"Who are you messaging?" Ria asked across the table.

"Oh no one, just catching up on messages."

"From Nina?" Ria asked.

"No no just you know, my mum, my sister."

"Cool. Ok well I'm gonna go and do a bit of shopping after this, if anyone fancies joining? Juliette?" Ria asked.

"Um, actually I think I'm gonna chill at the apartment after this."

Juliette replied:

What's your address?

10

Nina's apartment was incredible. It was a mezzanine penthouse with a rooftop overlooking Barcelona. This was a party pad alright. And it looked like Nina had had a party last night judging from the empty bottles by the door. Nina saw Juliette clock them.

"Listen baby. I had some friends back last night after the club. You disappeared so yeah I had some people over. But I promise you. I never tasted anyone else last night." She pulled Juliette to her and kissed her softly.

"Let's go to the bedroom." Juliette whispered to Nina. They walked up the staircase to the master bedroom. A huge circular bed, a bag of coke still on the bedside table. Nina pushed Juliette onto the bed and opened her drawer. She chucked a bag on the bed.

"My bag of tricks." She smiled. She stripped down and put on a strap on dildo with a black leather harness. "I'm going to fuck you now Juliette."

Juliette didn't need telling twice. She quickly stripped and spread her legs. Nina handcuffed her wrists to the headboard.

"Tell me how much you want me to fuck you." Nina asked.

"I want you to fuck me." Juliette replied.

Nina didn't move.

"Please." Juliette begged.

"I think maybe I'll sit on your face a bit first." She unclipped the harness and sat on Juliette's face. She could hardly breathe. She started to lick and suck, she felt something metal. A clit ring. Why was that such a turn on. She felt herself getting wetter. Nina felt her pussy.

"You like it when I dominate you." Nina said. "Good. Keep licking." She moaned, grinding into Juliette's face. Juliette was gasping. She was desperate to touch herself. To provide some relief. Nina dismounted, put the harness on and fucked Juliette with the strap on dildo. In and out it went. Gliding through her soaking pussy. Suddenly Juliette couldn't contain herself anymore. She came, squirting in the process. Nina quickly pulled out and began lapping up the juices. She buried her head into Juliette's crotch.

"Fuck me. I love it when girls squirt you know." She unclipped the harness and began rubbing her clit furiously. Moaning and licking until she came.

"I wanted to make you come." Juliette panted.

"You did. That fucking squirt sent me over the edge. You know how hard it is for me to come?" Nina lit a cigarette and walked over to the mezzanine balcony. It was 5pm.

"Shit I better go." Juliette said, hurriedly putting her clothes on. As she walked to the front door, it opened and a busty blonde entered.

"Who are you?" The woman asked Juliette in a strong German accent. Nina rushed down the stairs.

"Hi baby, this is my friend Juliette. She's Pablo's girlfriend. You know Pablo?"

"Oh yeah. Hi, I'm Madeline." She brushed past Juliette and kissed Nina, before opening the fridge and grabbing a beer.

"Nina you didn't get the food for tonight! You know we have my friends coming for dinner."

"Sorry baby I'll go out now ok. Come on Juliette I'll see you out."

Juliette was silent in the elevator. Nina was waiting for her to say something but she didn't.

"Bye Nina." Juliette said as they reached the foyer. And she went back to the apartment.

11

"Where have you been? I thought you said you were going back to the apartment?" Lauren asked.

"Yeah I did but then I needed to get some air and I just walked further than I realised. It all looks the same round here. You know the blocks. I got a coffee and then just walked you know. I mean I feel better for it but yeah sorry guys I lost track of time. I'll get showered really quickly and then let's go for drinks yeah? How was the beach?" She changed the subject as she raced to get ready.

"Hot and crowded. You didn't miss anything." Nancy called back.

After two big nights, the girls were pretty knackered. Regret hung in the air. Ria felt awkward about her and Juliette. Deep down she knew she'd been to see Nina and it killed her. Lauren being Lauren was pretending she didn't care that Pablo and Samuel hadn't messaged since *El Bitch*.

"Yeah so we'll probably hook up again tomorrow, or the day after or whatever. I'll definitely see them again before we go home anyway." Ria didn't get Lauren. If she wasn't her friend she'd be thinking badly of her. How could she just let guys use her like that and think she was the one in control of the situation. She felt sad for her. Inside Lauren just wanted to be loved. But she put on this act like she was '*one of the guys*'. She got into relationships quickly but they always ended quickly too. And the ones that had lasted had been a joke quite frankly. Ria didn't like girls who slept around and she was pretty sure a lot of guys thought the same. Lauren just wasn't girlfriend material. She'd never express that verbally of course. But she sure as hell thought it.

"*Más cava chicas?*" Nancy asked, filling up the girl's glasses. Nancy was oblivious to the sombre air in the room.

"Thirsty Juliette?" Lauren teased as Juliette drained her glass ready for a top up. Juliette was feeling bad about Ria. She'd instigated it after all but she knew Ria would be feeling awkward about it now. She needed to make more effort with her now, so she knew nothing had changed between them. But it had changed. And they both knew it deep down.

Juliette was wearing a new black leather dress. She felt more confident than usual and she couldn't help but think about Nina and how she'd love to show her what she was missing. Her figure was incredible. Ria thought she was the most beautiful girl she'd ever been with and it saddened her to think it wouldn't happen again. Juliette was girlfriend material. But Ria had never thought that could be a possibility until last night so she'd suppressed her feelings for the sake of their friendship. But now something had happened. And it was good. She wanted more. Why was forbidden love so much more exciting?

The girls rolled out into a cab to head to a tapas bar in *Gràcia*. It was Lauren's idea, which she claimed had nothing to do with the fact that that's where Samu lived.

In the cab, Ria felt Juliette's hand grip hers. She entwined her fingers into hers. Ria felt her heart pound before Juliette took her hand away and leant forward to chat to the taxi driver.

"Here's fine *Señor*." Juliette slurred.

The tapas bar Lauren had chosen was definitely more of a bar that did some tapas as opposed to a tapas restaurant. The quiet night was beginning to take a turn.

Juliette's phone was ringing. It was Nina. She cancelled the calls.

"Nina?" Ria asked. She couldn't help but look hurt.

"Yeah but I'm not answering Ria. There's nothing going on with us."

"Hey you don't have to explain yourself Juliette. You're a free agent."

"Yeah no course. I just don't want you think…well you know."

"I'm not sure I do. Do you even care what I think about who you're into?"

"Well I guess not no. Sorry. I won't mention it again." Ria felt angry with herself. But she was hurt. Really hurt. Juliette had come onto her. She ordered a shot and walked over to a group of girls at the bar and started chatting to them. Juliette looked over and took out her phone.

I'm in Gràcia. Want to meet?

Nina immediately started typing.

You know I want that pussy again.

Juliette felt her tummy go all funny. If a guy spoke to her like this she wouldn't be into it. But with Nina it was different.

Come and get it then.

She replied, sending her location.

Lauren and Nancy had ordered a bottle of cava and some tapas: padron peppers, tortilla, chorizo in a red wine sauce and some calamari. Juliette didn't feel like eating, she was too excited at the anticipation of having Nina eat her pussy again. She loved how much she loved it. Just the thought of it was making her wet. Ria seemed to be making some ground with the American girls she'd joined.

"I'm glad Ria's finally getting some attention." Nancy giggled.

"Mate, if I was a lesbian I would totally be into Ria. She's smoking. Right Jools?"

"Yeah of course. I mean she's gorgeous."

"I have to say Lauren I'm surprised you've not dabbled with a woman before?" Nancy teased. "You're so freaking horny."

"I have thought about it but I just love cock too much." She declared and the girls burst into fits of laughter. "But in all seriousness never say never. I guess it is on my bucket list. But not with Ria. That would be too weird. Can you imagine?" Juliette didn't say anything. She checked her phone to see if Nina had called. She hadn't. So she excused herself and went to the toilet.

By the time Nina walked into the tapas bar, the girls were on their fifth round of shots. Ria had been making out with a girl from Texas at the bar for the last hour. Nancy and Lauren had integrated themselves into a stag do and Juliette was waiting at the bar trying not to look desperate. Nina snuck up behind her and put her arms around her waist.

"Let's go." She whispered and led Juliette outside.

"Where are we going? I can't leave the girls without telling them." Juliette protested feebly.

"We can't go back to mine but Samu lives around the corner and he owes me a favour."

Nina and Juliette walked the five minutes to Samu's place. Nina had obviously contacted him on her way because he'd left her a key behind the bar next to his place. As soon as they got in the lift Nina began kissing Juliette's neck from behind. Juliette wished she had the strap on. The lift was completely mirrored and she wanted Nina to fuck her from behind so she could watch herself.

Inside Samuel's apartment Nina didn't hang about. She started stripping and Juliette followed suit. Naked, they stood in front of the floor to ceiling lounge window. They hungrily sucked each other's breasts. Nina had definitely had a boob job and Juliette was strangely turned on by the hard pertness of them. Nina pushed Juliette onto the couch, rubbing her beautiful olive skin all over Juliette's pure white body. Nina had a small black strip of hair on her vulva and a small gold hoop through her clit. She lined up her clit with Juliette's and began moving her hips rhythmically, rubbing their clits together so they were both red in the face. They came together, lying entangled on the sofa. Nina stroked her hair and kissed her shoulder.

"You sure you have to go home?" She asked Juliette.

"You have a girlfriend Nina." Juliette laughed, putting her clothes back on.

"It's complicated. Madeline is more business than pleasure shall we say."

"I'd say it's pretty straight forward Nina. She lives with you doesn't she. You have dinner parties together. You're a couple."

"Well I'm not at the dinner party am I? I'm here with you."

"That doesn't mean anything. I'll leave in a couple of days and you'll go back to your relationship until the next fling comes along." This really tickled Nina.

"You're right. I will go back to her. But there's a reason I always look elsewhere and a reason why I have to go back to her."

"Is she holding you at ransom?" Juliette retorted.

"Her dad is my boss Juliette. And he's not someone you want to get on the wrong side of. So like I said. It's complicated."

Juliette had never asked Nina what she did for a living. I think she's assumed it was something to do with the bar they'd gone to on the first night that her brother ran. But no one had an apartment like Nina's working in a bar.

"Are you a drug dealer Nina?" Juliette asked straight faced. Nina looked at Juliette for a while before she answered.

"Yes."

It was time to go and find the girls. Juliette felt like she was in a film. She'd gone to Barcelona for a girls holiday and ended up sleeping with two women – one her best friend and the other a Spanish drug dealer who was in a relationship with her boss's daughter.

"I need to go back and find the girls." Juliette smiled. This was definitely the last time she would see Nina again.

12

"Where have you been?" Nancy called across the bar as Juliette walked back in. This time, alone. Ria was nowhere to be seen. Maybe she'd taken the Texan back to the airbnb. Lauren was hammered. She was talking to a random girl crying that Pablo hadn't messaged her.

"Shit is Lauren ok?" Juliette asked.

"She's fine. Just drunk. But we should probably get her back. I think Ria's gone off with the cowgirl." Juliette and Nancy held Lauren up, walking her outside and hailing a cab.

"What's wrong with me?" Lauren was balling. Her mascara smudged under her eyes.

"Nothing, Lauren it was just a holiday romance. What would you do if Pablo text anyway? We've only got a couple more nights and then we go home." Juliette was reassuring her.

Back at the airbnb, Nancy made toast for Lauren and made her drink a pint of squash with some paracetamol. Meanwhile Ria had brought home Lacey, a Texan girl studying in Barcelona for a term. They'd been drinking in Ria's room but it hadn't progressed past a bit of kissing. Lacey was pretty drunk, and Ria really wasn't feeling it. Plus now she knew Juliette was back, she just wanted to be with her. She waited until Lacey had dozed off and crept out the bedroom to join the girls in the living room. By the time Ria had joined them, Lauren had crashed and Nancy was helping her to bed. Juliette and Ria were left alone.

"I heard you pulled." Juliette smiled. Ria exuded this effortless cool air about her. She was smart but never arrogant but above all she didn't care what people thought of her. She never followed the crowd. She knew who she was and what and whom she liked.

"Not really." Ria laughed, pouring a glass of water.

"Fancy a night cap?" Juliette asked.

Ria paused. She wanted to scream yes but she knew better.

"No, I'm pretty knackered. Just came out to get some water." She lied.

"Ok." Juliette said, entwining her hands in Ria's. Ria lent her forehead on Juliette's so their noses were touching and they could feel each other's breath.

"What are you doing Jools. It's not fair." Ria whispered.

Juliette didn't say anything. Just clasped her hands tighter into Ria's. Their lips touched and they kissed softly. It was a romantic kiss. For the first time, it was romantic over lustful. Juliette longed to feel Ria's skin against hers again. She felt terrible for going back to Nina. It was so unlike her. It all was. They parted with shy smiles and went to bed. Separately.

13

That morning, the girls ate breakfast as a five. Ria was hoping Lacey would make a sharp exit but she was keen to stick around.

"Pass me the OJ will you darlin'," she drawled.

"So Lacey, are you coming out with us tonight?" Nancy asked.

"No she can't." Ria snapped.

"Sure can." Lacey beamed. Seemingly unaware of Ria's response. It was a good hour before Ria managed to get her out the apartment, promising that she'd message with details of the plan for later that evening.

"Thanks a lot guys." Ria said, smiling but evidently pissed off. "That was the longest breakfast of my life."

"I thought you liked her Ri?" Lauren asked.

"Nothing happened. We just kissed, then she pretty much passed out. She was so pissed. Plus I don't even know her. I certainly don't want to spend another night with her. Jesus."

"Ok. Sor-rryyy" Lauren said. Just then Lauren's phone pinged. It was Pablo.

Hey sexy lady. You want to come to a party at Samu's tonight? But I don't want to share you this time.

Lauren couldn't help but smile.

I'm not a booty call Pablo.

She replied teasingly.

You could never be a booty call. I'm in London next week and I want to see you then too. This doesn't have to end if you don't want it to.

Lauren couldn't hide the smile from her face. She replied:

What's his address?

For the rest of the day, Lauren couldn't stop talking about Pablo and how '*they just got one another*'. She was going to go shopping to buy something special to wear for the evening. Ria, Nancy and Juliette were going to visit *La Sagrada Familia* and *Parc Güell*. They'd meet back up at the apartment to get ready around fiveish.

As soon as the girls had left, Lauren messaged Pablo.

Free apartment if you want to make it up to me?

Give me half an hour :)

Lauren jumped into the shower to freshen up. Then changed into a skirt and tank top and lay in wait. For once Pablo was on time. She buzzed him up and they began making out as soon as he walked in the door. Pablo bent down to put his head under Lauren's skirt. He was pleasantly surprised to find she wasn't wearing any knickers. A soft hairless mound greeted him. He nuzzled his nose into her slit. Up and down he rubbed as she moaned softly. He inserted his tongue expertly, rooting around until she opened her legs to let him taste inside. She moaned in relief and he stuffed his hand down his boxers to release his throbbing member from its prison.

"Just fuck me." She begged, panting.
Pablo ignored her, using his hands to push her down onto the chair and spread her wide so he could drive her even more wild with his tongue. Lauren arched her back.

"You're going to make me come." She moaned, flushing red.

Pablo stopped immediately. Rising up he took out his sizable cock with his right hand. His circumcised bell glistened with pre cum.

"Please" She begged, drawing him closer so he could insert himself.

He obliged. Teasingly he dipped his cock into her. In and out. In and out. The whole way in so she could feel the full thickness of the base but slow enough so she was continuously on the edge of climax. Lauren started to rub her clit, desperate to come but Pablo stopped her, withdrawing completely. He stood before her, an adonis. A ripped tanned physique. Like a gladiator she thought. Beneath those baggy clothes he had the body of a god. He started to jerk himself off, periodically rubbing his bell end into her clit and dipping the tip into her wet pussy. She started to play with herself, sitting up so she could suck his cock. He held her hair, trapping his cock in her mouth so she gagged - but she loved it. The harder she sucked the more she fingered herself. Her thighs were sodden with juices. Suddenly her mouth was filled with warm cum and as she felt the rush of his climax she came herself. Turned on by the suffocation of his cock.

14

Juliette was feeling nervous about going back to Samuel's. As far as the others were concerned, she'd never been there before. What if Samuel mentioned something? And what if Nina was there?

Lauren pressed the buzzer and a random guy wearing sunglasses opened the door to let them in. The flat was packed. There must have been at least fifty people there already. Someone was DJing on the decks, there was a drinking game going on around the dining table, and a load of people outside smoking pot.

"*Mi amor!*" Pablo said, holding Lauren's hands and kissing her tenderly on the mouth. He draped his arm over her shoulders and took her through to meet his friends outside.

"*Chicas* help yourself to drink yeah. In the kitchen ok." Samuel shouted as he walked through with a mirrored tray of cocaine, which he laid out on the coffee table.

Just then Juliette clocked Nina and Madeline on the terrace. Her heart was in her stomach.

"Pick me up?" She asked Ria and Nancy. The trio headed to the coffee table and each did a line.

"You're going to have to wean yourself off this when you're home Juliette." Nancy laughed. "Never seen you like this before."

Juliette looked bashful.

"Ah I just feel nervous at these things you know. Plus it's better here. Not like the shit you get in London. I don't feel too bad the next day." She tried to convince herself.

"Yeah, I know what you mean. Although I can't say I've been feeling my best here." Nancy said.

"We're on holiday. Don't sweat it." Ria smiled.

Juliette wanted to reach out for Ria. She was such a good person. How could she mess her about like this.

"Hello ladies." Nina called as she walked in from the terrace with Madeline.

"My better half Madeline." She announced.

Ria's jaw gaped.

"You have a girlfriend? Wow, ok." Ria scoffed. Nina looked like she wanted to murder her.

"Don't tell me." Madeline said dead pan. "You fucked her and thought she was single?" She made a mock sad face. "You're not the first one and you won't be the last." She rolled her eyes as she unscrewed her pendant to reveal a small spoon of coke which she sniffed as casually as if she was blowing her nose. She scooped a second spoon from her necklace and held it out to Ria.

"Compensation." She smiled.

"No thanks." Ria retorted. "And for your information, I didn't get with Nina and I never would."

"Ah, so it's you. Pablo's girlfriend." Madeline locked eyes with Juliette.

Juliette wanted the ground to swallow her. She could see Lauren and Pablo making out in the corner. Nina's cover for her was about to blow.

"Pablo's girlfriend?" Nancy asked confused. "It's Lauren that's getting with Pablo, not Juliette."

"Ladies, this is sooo boring." Nina smiled. "Who wants a drink?"

"Did you fuck the milk bottle Nina?" Madeline asked.

"Baby what? Nooo this is so silly. You are the only one I'm fucking. If you still want me to of course." She cocked her head to the side and Madeline waltzed off, not angry but not happy either. She liked to keep Nina on her toes, but ultimately she believed what she wanted to. And Madeline wanted to believe that Nina was all hers.

Juliette decided this was a good time to leave too. She grabbed Nancy and went outside to see Lauren and Pablo.

"You've had your fun. Now fuck off." Nina sneered at Ria. "Don't think I don't notice how you look at Juliette. She's not interested in you. It's embarrassing watching how pathetic you are around her. You've known her what? 15 years. And she still doesn't want you. I've known her for five minutes and she can't get enough of me." She leant in and whispered "I can fuck her whenever I want. And guess what? I will. I'm not done with her Ria. Just because you're going back to London, this isn't the last you'll hear of me." She walked off smirking, leaving Ria shaking with anger. She wanted to scream that Nina was wrong. That Juliette did like her. But she knew if it came out in that way, Juliette might be spooked into ending whatever it was between them. She also felt humiliated. Clearly Juliette had been with Nina more than once. How could they have something more special than her and Juliette?

Juliette's phone buzzed.

Your friend nearly fucked things up for us. Control her.

Juliette flushed red as she typed.

Is that a threat Nina?

No. A caution.

Juliette was raging. Who did Nina think she was. She replied.

Don't fucking speak to me like that Nina. Go fuck yourself.

"*Chupitos*!" Samuel called as he handed out shots of tequila. Juliette downed two, slamming the plastic cups back onto the tray. As she looked up she saw Nina, looking furious. She gripped Juliette's arm, whispering in her ear.

"Outside."

She followed her into Samuel's bedroom and outside onto his bedroom terrace. Nina locked the bedroom door so no one would come in. Nina looked Juliette up and down. She was shaking with anger. Juliette felt scared but strangely turned on. Nina held Juliette by the neck with one hand as she slipped her other hand up her dress and into her pants.

"How did I fucking guess you'd be turned on by this."
They both smiled, kissing passionately as Nina slipped in
two fingers, finger fucking her hard as she moaned and
writhed against the wall. Nina held one hand over her
mouth to muffle her screams of ecstasy as she finished
what she started and brought her to climax.

"We can't keep doing this Nina." Juliette whispered.
"People are going to get hurt."

"Don't worry about Madeline. It will be easier once
you're not in the same city. She's going back to Berlin
next week for a month and you're going back to London
soon. So you won't have to see each other."

"What do you mean easier? Whatever this is, it's over
when I get on that plane Nina. I'm not about to get
caught in a lesbian love triangle."
Nina cackled.

"You are so funny with your words Juliette."

"I'm serious Nina. This is a holiday thing. When I go
home, I'm going back to my boring old life." Juliette went
to leave the room but Nina stopped her.

"I'm gonna be on the first flight to London once
Madeline leaves for Berlin." And then she let her go.

15

Nancy had lost Lauren to Pablo, Juliette was nowhere to be seen and Ria was chatting shit high on coke to some gay guys. She decided to make a French exit. But just as she was about to leave she clocked a familiar face. Juan Felipe. The yoga instructor from *Shakti Move*. She didn't expect him to remember her but he was making his way over. He was wearing a tie-dye shirt with a yin and yang symbol on, striped yoga pants and...he was barefoot bar an anklet.

"Miss Nancy." He smiled, kissing her on both cheeks.

"Juan Felipe, I wasn't expecting to see you here."

"Well of course. Why would you? I met Samuel in the Gili Islands many moons ago. Now fate has brought us together again. In Barcelona."

"Are you from here originally?" She asked.

"Where are any of us really from Nancy?" He asked, but Nancy had the impression she wasn't actually meant to answer.

"Yeah sure...I just meant did you grow up here?"

"I am still growing." He smiled serenely.

Cool. This was going well. He was literally talking in riddles.

"Where did you go to school?" She tried.

"I went to school in La Coruña. I'm from the north originally but after my studies I spent a few years in India, Indonesia, South East Asia..." he waved his hand as if more places followed but didn't elaborate.

"Where did you go in India? I spent some time there myself."

"Kerala mostly. Hempey. Goa a bit. I'm a water sign. I need to be close to the water. And you are..." He closed his eyes again as if reading her fortune. "Earth...Taurus."

"How did you know?" Nancy didn't really believe in star signs but she couldn't help but feel impressed that Juan Felipe could read her so well as to know hers.

"I'm a very spiritual person Nancy." He said rolling a joint. "I don't usually smoke...I prefer to ingest in oil form. It's the most pure. But at a party. I make exceptions." He winked, lighting it up and taking a drag.

"Do you smoke?" He asked, offering her the joint. She took it from him and took a drag. There was something about him she really liked. He had a calming presence that on paper would be annoying. But he was charming, boyishly good looking but not arrogant and she respected the fact he was passionate about what he did. He hadn't conformed to the norms. They were polar opposites in so many ways but there was obviously something that drew them together. He seemed interested in her. Curious. And she in turn was curious about him too.

"Do you want to get out of here?" She asked, surprising herself.

"I thought you'd never ask." He nodded, smiling like a happy Buddha, a little bit stoned but still in control.

They headed to Juan Felipe's flat. A loft apartment he shared with two artists, who were currently in Paris helping to set up an exhibition for a friend. It was dark, and the windows needed a good wash but it was full of plants and a strong smell of incense. Indian music played from the radio in the kitchen and a dahl bubbled away in the slow cooker. Juan Felipe took off his top and laid on his bed, a mattress on the floor, and started to roll another joint. Nancy browsed his bookshelf. It was almost entirely made up of titles about Buddhism, yoga, meditation, astrology and magic. There were also a few vegan cookery books, and some travel guides. Nancy always thought a bookshelf said a lot about the person they belonged to. Apart from the books on magic, she expected the rest, although magic certainly wasn't off topic for the type of person Juan Felipe was. She lay next to him on the bed. Silently, they passed each other the joint, blissing out to the sound of the sitar on the radio. She wasn't sure who made the first move, but when the joint was finished they began kissing. Delicate romantic kisses. There was no foreplay. Like a teenager, Juan Felipe rushed to the sex part. He lay on top of her in missionary, rhythmically thrusting as if to the music. But he was so good looking, Nancy could forgive him. Afterwards she lay with her head his armpit. It smelt of essential oils. And she held his hand that draped around her, feeling his fingers and the textures of the various rings he wore. She couldn't say it was the best sex of her life...but she felt fulfilled. She felt loved and nourished almost. Like she'd had a home cooked supper.

16

Lauren and Pablo had snuck into Samuel's brother's room.

"I've never met a girl like you before." Pablo sat on the bed and looked up at Lauren as she stripped down to her thong. She was womanly. With curves in all the right places. Just how Pablo liked it.

"Is that a good thing?" Lauren giggled, hooking her finger into her thong string and pulling it up so Pablo could catch a glimpse of the goods.

"I'd say it's a very good thing." He pulled her on top of him and she grinded herself into his crotch. She felt him grow hard beneath his jeans but she kept on grinding. Enjoying the friction of the rough jeans against her clit. They kissed passionately. A knock on the door.

"Fuck off!" Pablo shouted. They continued. Two bodies entwined, kissing and pressing themselves against one another. But their underwear stayed on and Lauren felt a rush as she climaxed. Her whole body felt warm and tingly. Waves of ecstasy rolling through her. They breathed heavily. Their faces pushed together.

"I can't wait to see you in London." Pablo whispered.

Ria had lost count of how much coke she'd had. She splashed her face with water in the bathroom and stared at herself in the mirror. Fuck. She never lost her head with girls. And she never lost herself to drugs. She was never messy. But the reflection in the mirror said otherwise.

"Have you seen Nancy?" Ria asked wide eyed to Samuel as she bumped into him coming out the bathroom.

"I think she left with Juan Felipe."

"Who? The yoga teacher? You have got to be kidding me." She huffed, marching over to the sofa to snatch up her bag. "Lauren?" She yelled over the music. But Lauren was too busy snogging Pablo to answer. She held her hand up as if to say bye.

"See you tomorrow." Ria said and left the flat.

She sat outside on the curb fumbling for her lighter. A joint. That's what she needed to come down a bit. If only she had a valium.

"Hey." Ria looked up. It was Juliette.

"I can't do it Juliette." Ria began to sob.

"I'm sorry. I'm really sorry. Can we just go back to how things were?" Juliette pleaded.

"I need time. It's fucked with my head man."

"I know. It has mine too." Juliette whispered. She wanted to hold Ria in her arms and make it all better. Was it possible to lust after two people? With Nina, it was all about the sex but with Ria...with Ria it was everything. She was everything. But Nina had this power over her. She went to jelly just at the thought of her. Maybe when they were back in London, and Nina was out of the picture, she could make a go of things with Ria? But did she even want that? Her mind was scrambled. Too much coke, too much tequila. She took a drag of Ria's joint.

"Let's go home Ri." And she hailed a cab.

When they got back to the apartment Nancy was already in bed. Ria was the drunkest Juliette had ever seen her. She kept trying to hold Juliette's hand.

"I want to Ria but I can't. It isn't fair on you."

"Once more isn't going to make a difference." She learnt in and Juliette reciprocated but she couldn't help but imagine Nina. She pushed Ria's head down into her crotch and imagined it was Nina taking those hungry licks. She moaned, forgetting where she was. On the sofa at the airbnb. Every time Ria tried to come up to kiss her, she pushed her head back down, writhing and moaning until she squirted hot liquid. An explosion. The best orgasm she'd ever had.

As she opened her eyes to pull her pants up she saw Nancy stood in the doorway. No one said a word.

"OK. Wow." Nancy was speechless. Juliette flushed red.

"Oh god. Nancy. I'm sorry."

"Why are you apologising? How long's this been going on?"

"Erm…it's not going on. It's…God I don't know. We were just drunk." Juliette offered.

"Ria?" Nancy asked.

"It's only happened a couple of times. But Juliette's right, it's not going anywhere. It shouldn't have happened. The last thing we want to do is make it awkward for anyone. Are you going to tell Lauren?"

"It's not for me to tell. I won't say a thing. But just be careful ok? I don't want anyone to get hurt." She said, closing her door, and Juliette had the distinct impression that that last comment was aimed solely at her.

"I better go to bed." Juliette said, squeezing Ria's hand and trailing into her bedroom. Ria sat on the sofa and cried. This was the worst comedown ever.

17

The next morning, Ria stood on the terrace overlooking Barcelona. Some fucked up trip this had turned out to be. She was mad with herself but she was madder with Juliette. Not only did she now have even stronger feelings for her, but now Nancy knew and it was only a matter of time before Lauren would find out and then their whole group would be changed forever.

"Penny for your thoughts?" Nancy sidled up beside her.

"I'm getting too old for this." Ria smiled, sipping her coffee. "I'm actually looking forward to getting on that plane. Back to the flat. You know?"

"Yeah it's been a heavy few days. But we've still got two more left. You shouldn't wish your time away Ri." Nancy cocked her head to the side. She really felt for Ria. Clearly she had feelings for Juliette. She wasn't sure exactly what had happened between Juliette and Nina but there was obviously something going on there too. And somewhere, Ria was caught up in the middle of it.

"Why don't you come to this yoga class with me this morning. We can go for some brunch together after. Just you and me. Leave Lauren and Juliette to nurse their heads."

"I honestly don't think I'd be able to Nancy. You have no idea how sick I feel. Not sure down dog's going to help."

"OK. Well walk with me. The fresh air will do you good. I'll only be an hour. Grab an orange juice somewhere. Take your book. And I'll meet you after." Ria didn't say anything. "I'm serious Ri, don't wait for her to wake up. Let's go." She led Ria in from the terrace and then headed out together. Careful to close the door quietly so as not to wake the others.

"So you like this guy then?" Ria smiled. Nancy blushed.

"I just fancy a morning stretch." She smiled. "And yeah I guess it would be nice to see him again. He's different from my usual type."

"That a good thing?"

"Well the others didn't exactly work out well did they? What's your type anyway? I have to say I never expected you and Juliette."

"Bloody hell Nance. Nice segway." Nancy laughed.

"Look I'm not asking for the details...to be honest I heard and saw quite a bit. I'm just surprised I guess. Lauren sure. But Juliette?! I'm telling you it's always the quiet ones."

"Ah I don't want to talk about it. Sorry. It's messed a bit with my head and I really don't want it to. Tell me about Juan Felipe." Ria said prolonging the name with an accentuated Spanish accent.

"OK well he has this...this aura. You know? This energy that I'm just drawn to. And you know that's not me at all. I'm a facts woman. I don't believe in all this fate and star signs bullshit. I mean the guy reads books about magic for fuck sake. But...I'm drawn to him. What can I say?"

Ria left Nancy at the yoga studio to find a quiet spot in the shade to scroll her phone mindlessly. There was no point in trying to read her book with this hangover. Nancy practically ran up the stairs to the door. Wanky dick face was there as usual.

"I'm here for the class." Nancy announced.

"It's full." He replied not even looking up from his book.

"Is Juan Felipe teaching?" At this the man put his book down and let out a long sigh.

"Yes he is teaching today but just because you fucked him it does not mean preferential treatment. Please book online to avoid disappointment." Nancy felt herself redden.

"How dare you speak to me like that you fucking shit." It was louder than she intended and suddenly the door to the studio was flung upon by none other than Juan Felipe.

"Nancy?" He looked shocked. "What is going on?"

"What's going on? Well why don't you tell me what's going on? I've just arrived for the class to be told that 'just because you fucked him it does not mean preferential treatment'. Is this what you do huh? Shag all your students. You're disgusting." And with that she turned on her heel and fled down the stairs before bursting into tears. For the next two hours, Nancy and Ria wandered the streets of Barcelona venting, crying, laughing and finally stopping for a beer in the sunshine.

"Why is it that more alcohol is the only cure for too much alcohol?" Ria pondered.

"I couldn't do wine now. It needs to be beer or a bloody mary for me."

"God no. I couldn't think of anything worse than a glass of wine now."

"I cannot believe I fell for his spiritual act. I bet he uses those lines all the time. A conveyor belt of shags with unsuspecting tourists. You know what's the most humiliating thing? He didn't even come after me."

"Stop torturing yourself Nancy. It's done. Fuck Juan Felipe."

"Fuck Juan Felipe." They chinked glasses and savoured the bitter taste in their mouths.

18

Juliette woke up in a world of regret. She crept in to speak to Ria but found she had gone. So had Nancy. Lauren was fast asleep next to a snoring Pablo. So she showered and headed out. She told herself she was going nowhere in particular but after a couple of blocks she messaged Nina.

I can't stop thinking about you.

No reply.

Can I see you?

Nothing. She carried on walking in the vague direction of Nina's penthouse. Suddenly her phone buzzed.

"Nina?"

"Where are you?"

"About a block from yours."

"Stay there and text me your address."

Ten minutes later Nina arrived in a cab.

"Get in." She instructed. Juliette did as she was told. Nina spoke rapidly in Spanish to the taxi driver.

"Where are we going?"

"My brother's bar. We can talk there. It's empty."

Juliette had forgotten where the bar was exactly. It looked different in the day. Nina opened up with a large set of keys, disabled the alarm and fixed them both a drink. Juliette walked towards her and put her arms around her neck.

"What did you want to talk about?" Juliette asked, lifting off her top. Her boobs looked fantastic in the bralet she was wearing. She started to unbutton her shorts. Nina sat on the bar stool stroking her crotch.

"How about you do a little dance for me." She asked twizzling Juliette around.

"I need to be drunk for that." Juliette said shyly. Nina produced a bag of white powder.

"Or high?" She asked chucking it on the floor. Juliette picked it up and dabbed her pinky in to dab some onto her gums and snort a little. Juliette began to dance. Her body took over. She was turning into a professional lap dancer. Where had this even come from? Nina was loving it. Smacking her ass as she bent over to push herself into

Nina's breasts and face. Nina pushed her onto all fours and began licking her pussy from behind. Juliette was moaning. This is what she was picturing when Ria was eating her out last night. She was picturing Nina's lightning tongue effortlessly flitting over her clit and pussy lips, poking deep inside her intermittently. Abruptly Nina got up and led Juliette through to the back of the room. She pushed a panel and a secret door swung open.

"What is this?" Juliette giggled, looking around at the soft seating, beds, whips, sex toys and a St Andrews cross on the wall with leather cuffs at each end.

"The playroom." Nina replied, closing the door. She led Juliette over by the hand and turned her so she faced the cross before cuffing her in. Juliette waited in anticipation. She felt her juices drip onto her leg.

"Nina?" She called.

Nina gripped her neck and moved a hard, freezing cold object across the top of her thighs and bum.

"Ready to be fucked now?" She asked as she plunged her ice cold glass strap on inside her. Juliette was in ecstasy. She loved the cold hardness of the glass. She wanted to touch Nina. To suck her tits. She thought about Nina sitting on her face as she buried her head into the wall. And she thought of Ria, and her beautiful body. Nina withdrew and began to lick her asshole. This was new territory.

"Nina." She giggled.

"Can I plug you?" Nina asked, showing Juliette a small silver bullet with a jewelled end.

"Will it hurt?" Juliette asked unsure.

"No, it will make the orgasm so much more intense. Trust me." She rubbed the butt plug inside Juliette's pussy to lubricate it before inserting it into her asshole. Then she bent down to lick her pussy, knowing that Juliette would be desperate for a better angle but restricted by the cross she had to take what she could get.

"Nina please." Juliette gasped. "Make me come." Nina withdrew and began to slowly strum her clit. Slow, unexpected motions to bring Juliette to the brink. Then she reinserted her strap on and let Juliette release herself in waves of orgasm.

When it was all over, Juliette realised it was gone lunch time. Staff would be arriving to ready the club for the evening.

"We better go." Juliette smiled at Nina.

"I'm gonna hang on. Got some business to attend to." Nina said, putting the room back together.

"It's my penultimate night tonight." Juliette said, leaning her forehead on Nina's.

"I know. I'll see you tomorrow before you go." She smiled. "You know Ria likes you don't you?"

"What?" Juliette blushed. "Don't be silly. We've been friends for years."

"Hmm. I don't like to be played Juliette. You don't want me as an enemy." She winked but Juliette was unsure whether she was being serious or not. As she went to leave she noticed the security cameras blinking red.

"Nina, the cameras?"

Nina laughed, "Don't worry, I'm going to wipe them. I'll see you tomorrow."

19

Lauren and Pablo spent the entire day in bed. Lauren felt like a teenager again. Constantly kissing, and rubbing their bodies against one another under the duvet. Every so often she'd duck under the covers to suck him off and he'd reciprocate, fingering her till she was soaking and begging for his cock to finish. They'd fuck loudly and lay in each others arms exhausted. Then they'd watch funny youtube videos, smoke a joint and order food. She wanted to stay in this exact loop forever.

"Tell me about London?" Pablo asked.

"What do you mean? You've been before."

"Yeah but I mean your London. What is a typical day in the life of Lauren…" He trailed off realising he didn't even know her surname.

"Oh my god you brute." She whacked him playfully.

"You've forgotten my name haven't you?" She eyed him accusingly.

"Lauren…Sexy? Lauren…Hot stuff? Lauren…Gives the best blowjobs?"

She nuzzled into him giggling before kissing his chest and making her way down to his boxers. He inched them down and took out his throbbing cock. She could literally see it growing in his hands. She began to lick the bell end. It drove him wild and she loved it. She held eye contact and licked from the base to the tip before swallowing it whole, using both hands at the same time. He was in ecstasy, exploding into her mouth. She gulped his cum hungrily.

Juliette was the first to arrive back. She'd taken the long route home, enjoying just being in Barcelona, people watching, getting a coffee and imagining what it would be like if she actually lived here permanently. God her life in London was going to take some readjusting to. She was already dreading going back into the office. When she arrived back she could hear Lauren and Pablo going at it. So she took herself onto the terrace and for the first time since she was at Uni, smoked a cigarette and pretended in that moment this was her flat, her life.

Ria and Nancy were making their way back when they saw signs for the Picasso Museum.

"Fancy it?" Ria asked.

"When in Rome."

They both saw themselves as creative people. Ria had recently started her own online clothing brand and was instrumental in the design process. Nancy was an analyst, she had always been motivated by being financially independent, but outside her day job she loved to experiment with fashion and interiors.

"It's incredible isn't it." *What was that accent? Dutch? Scandinavian?* "It's one of the most important paintings when it comes to understanding Picasso's evolution into cubism."

"I'm afraid I can't reciprocate with anything meaningful." Nancy said smiling. "I'm doing the obligatory tourist bucket list. Of course I appreciate what's in front of me, but I couldn't say how individual pieces have shaped art movements let alone their hidden meanings."

The man chuckled.

"I appreciate your honesty. I'm Henrik." He held out his hand.

"Nancy." They stood in silence in front of the painting.

"Nancy. This is my number. If you happen to be at a loose end one evening, I would love to take you out for dinner." He handed her a business card and left.

Dr. Henrik Hansen

Ria rushed over. She'd seen the interaction unfold but kept her distance.

"He was hot." She exclaimed. "And that really is saying something coming from me."

"He was...tall." Nancy laughed.

"Nance, he looked like a film star." She grabbed the business card. "Fuck me, he owns a gallery?"

"It doesn't say he's the owner." Nancy rolled her eyes and stuffed the card into her bag.

"Er his surname is Hansen...the same name as the gallery."

"I'm sure it's a common name. It doesn't mean he's the owner Ria."

"Well if he doesn't own it, I bet his family does. You are going to message him right?"

"Ah I dunno. I think one failed holiday romance is enough for me."

"Nancy?" Ria looked at her with wide eyes.

"OK I'll message. But not now. Don't want to appear too keen. Jesus." She linked arms with Ria and they walked around the remainder of the gallery.

20

"Never thought I'd say this but I think next year we should maybe do something more...chilled. Spa weekend, New York galleries. Anything that doesn't involve copious amounts of drink and drugs basically." Ria said as Lauren poured glasses of *sangria*.

"Cheers. To our penultimate night." Lauren said as the girls chinked their glasses on the terrace.

"I'm with Ria. This has been like a bloody stag do." Said Nancy.

"Well I for one have enjoyed the stag do. And I think Juliette has too." Juliette blushed.

"Yeah, maybe a little too much." She offered, avoiding eye contact with Ria and Nancy.

"So Juliette, we're all dying to know. Clearly something's going on between you and Nina. Are you going to be tearing up Soho with Ria when we're home?" Nobody spoke. "What? What did I say?" Said Lauren.

"Nothing's going on with Nina." Juliette said finally. "She has a girlfriend. And…I'm not gay."

Ria went inside, quickly followed by Nancy under the illusion of fetching a bottle of cava. Luckily for them, Lauren was far more interested in talking about herself anyway. So the conversation naturally took a turn to her and Pablo.

"The thing with Pablo is…and trust me you'll get it when you meet someone Jools. He just gets me, you know? Like we genuinely have so much fun together. We just laugh." Juliette was happy to keep fueling this conversation. Anything to take the heat off of her.

"You going to text Hot Hansen then?" Ria asked as she grabbed the cava glasses from the cupboard.

"Yeah, I cannot listen to Lauren bang on about Pablo all night. Hate to leave you in the lurch Ri but I'm going to see if he fancies a drink."

Hi Henrik, it was nice to meet you earlier.

No no too formal.

Hey Henrik, are you free this evening?

Ria grabbed the phone and typed:

Hey Henrik, the girls and I are heading into town shortly. If you fancy a drink let me know and I'll send our location.

Nancy's phone pinged back almost immediately.

Hello Nancy, I wasn't holding up much hope to hear from you but I'm glad I have. I'm with a client in El Borne but I'll be free afterwards. Would you like to meet for dinner? I know a great Argentinian place.

Nancy couldn't hide the smile from her face. Ria replied:

That sounds great. Where and when?

"Ria! You know how desperate that's going to make me seem?"

"Nancy you need to skip the bullshit. You want to go for dinner. So does he. Why go around the houses?"

"Ah it's just not very appealing is it? Guys like girls to be hard to get Ria. You wouldn't know." She smirked.

"Well as someone who is interested in women...the ones that play hard to get are never the ones you want to settle down with."

"Hmm, sounds like you might want to take your own advice there Ri." She said, nodding over to Juliette who was engrossed in conversation with Lauren.

"Well we all make mistakes." Ria smiled, sipping her drink.

"And is that what it was? Is? A mistake?"

"Well I'm pretty sure she's been sleeping with Nina so yeah I'd say it was definitely a mistake. But I didn't know that. So…" She trailed off in thought.

"Sorry Ri." Nancy said, smiling sympathetically. The awkwardness was quickly brushed over as Nancy's phoned pinged.

I've booked a table at La Cabrera in El Borne for 9pm :)

Invigorated by the cava she replied instantly.

Great. See you then.

"Better get ready." She tottered off into the bedroom to change. A midi black knit dress. Fitted to show off her physique and make her bouncy red curls pop. She appeared on the terrace just after 8.30pm to announce her departure.

"Right I'm off kids. Don't do anything I wouldn't do."

21

Nancy arrived at *La Cabrera* just after half past eight. It was a tiny Argentinian restaurant with about eight tables of two. The walls were exposed stone, lit up by candles. It was romantic. Henrik was sat at the back browsing a wine menu. He was dressed casually in turned up chinos and a white cotton t-shirt that showed off his tanned toned arms. His long blonde hair slicked back. When he saw her he stood up immediately to kiss her on both cheeks and pull out her chair.

"Nancy you look beautiful." He smiled. "Is the Malbec Finca Altamira Mendoza ok for you?"
Nancy had no idea what that was.

"Perfect." She smiled back as he ordered in perfect Spanish with the waiter. "This looks like a lovely restaurant. Have you been here before?"

"I have taken a client here before. The steak is really very good. You do like steak?" He asked, suddenly panicked.

"Oh yes I love steak. There's nothing I don't eat really." God she was definitely being too eager here. "Apart from black olives." She added as an afterthought. "But I don't mind them in sauces." Wow she sounded like a real nerd. The waiter returned to pour their wine.

"So you're into cooking?" Henrik asked.

"Yes I do enjoy cooking. Mainly savoury, I'm not much of a baker. I tend to cook Asian dishes. Sushi, curries, a bit of a mix really. And you?" She said taking a sip of the wine. "Wow this is delicious." *Christ he better be paying for this.*

"It's a very good wine yes. Actually I don't cook very much. I'm away a lot so I eat out mostly. When I'm home I have a very simple diet. Salads, fish, meat mostly." Why did everything Henrik say sound so intelligent and considered.

"And where is home?"

"I'm based in London at the moment. The gallery there is being renovated so there is a lot of work to be done. And you?"

"London also." Nancy smiled. "Clapham."

"Of course." He smiled. "I think this is a very popular place at the moment? I myself am in Shepherds Market."

"Mayfair?"

"Yes it is not exactly where I would choose but it was my father's place. When he died I wanted to keep it in the family. Of course I have changed it a lot since I moved in."

"I'm so sorry. Did he die recently?"

"No no it's quite alright. He was ill for a long time. He died five years ago now. I do not dwell on it."

"And so the gallery is a family business?"

"Yes my grandfather Henrik Hansen, the first, founded the gallery after the war. It started in Copenhagen and my father opened the New York Gallery with his father. Then I opened the London gallery with mine. One day if I have a son I hope to open the next one in Tokyo with him."

"Wow, that's incredible. I can't say my family history is nearly as exciting." The waiter came over to take their orders. Henrik ordered a selection of empanadas to share followed by fillet steaks with potato gratin, creamed spinach and sweetcorn. Nancy found herself hypnotised by Henrik's accent. She listened attentively to his life in Denmark, his commitment to the galleries and his passion for travel. He was so cultured, so intelligent, so interesting. He in turn was impressed with her degree from Cambridge. He himself had studied at Harvard before doing a masters at Oxford. He was also impressed by how much she'd travelled alone, laughing at her misfortunes travelling through Central America with a broken foot and how she nearly got shipwrecked on route to Komodo Island. By the time the food and wine was finished it was gone eleven. They'd chatted non-stop and Nancy found herself relaxing in his company. Henrik insisted on paying the bill and walking Nancy to a cab.

"I would love to see you again." He said sincerely looking into her eyes.

"Me too. I've had a wonderful evening Henrik. Thank you." Their eyes met and they kissed in the doorway of a shuttered up shop.

"Is it terribly impolite of me to ask if you'd like to come back to my hotel room for a drink?"

She smiled, "A drink?" She said making quotation marks with her fingers. He laughed and they kissed again, this time more passionately and Nancy felt butterflies in her stomach.

They took a taxi to the W hotel where Henrik had a penthouse suite with floor to ceiling glass sea views. They tumbled onto the bed. Nancy slipped out of her dress. She'd chosen not to wear any underwear so she stood before him with two erect nipples and a mound of red hair on her vulva. She helped him remove his t-shirt and unbuttoned his trousers to unleash his member. He laid back on the bed as she sucked his long hard penis and he sighed in pleasure. He loved seeing her peachy bum bob up and down as she moved with the view of the waves behind her. Nancy pulled herself on top of Henrik and used the wet tip of his penis to rub her clit. She moaned, throwing her head back before he pulled her on top of him to feel her body against his. He kissed her passionately, holding her with his strong arms. She pulled back and straddled him, his cock resting erect on her navel. He could feel her wet pussy dripping onto his legs. She lifted herself up and sat on his cock, moaning as the inches went deeper and deeper. Was there nothing this guy didn't have. She rode his rock hard cock and he spread her ass cheeks to allow her pussy to take more. She moaned and buried her head into his chest and he lifted her ass up and down so he could fuck her even faster. He came hard, filling her with hot cum as he sucked her breasts.

When he'd caught his breath he led her into the shower, kissing her passionately. He pushed her against the marble wall as the warm water rained down on them both. Her tits looked fantastic. Two pert teardrops glistening with soapy water. Henrik felt his cock harden. He wanted to fuck her again but first it was time to taste that sweet pussy. They dried off and he led her back into the bedroom, pushing her down onto the bed. He spread her legs and licked slowly, moaning into her as he stroked his throbbing member at the same time. He was panting hard moving his hand up and down his shaft in quick motions. Nancy couldn't believe he was already ready to go again.

"You're so hot." He moaned, as he moved his hand quickly over his cock whilst licking her pussy at the same time. Nancy loved how turned on he was by her.

"Fuck me again." She moaned. He stood up and angled his cock into her sodden lips. She was so wet, his cock was quickly lubricated. She wanted to watch it glide in and out of her but the angle was wrong so she closed her eyes and imagined that hard Danish cock fucking her. That rich hard cock pounding her pussy. She started to rub her clit, getting off at the thought of how rich and successful Henrik was. She'd never fucked a guy this powerful before and she loved it. Henrik was clearly loving the show. He withdrew to taste her once more and as he did she came on his tongue and he finished himself off, covering his stomach in his own cum.

22

Juliette, Ria and Lauren had decided to try one of the local restaurants on the street of their airbnb. Every time they'd walked past it there was a huge queue which was usually a good sign. The window display was full of fresh seafood and towers of oysters but their main speciality was '*flautas*', small thin baguettes filled with everything from iberico ham to urchins. The restaurant didn't take bookings, so they wandered down to join the queue. There was an air of tension between Ria and Juliette and without Nancy, it was hard hiding it from Lauren.

"You guys are quiet tonight?" Lauren pressed.

"Knackered mate." Ria smiled, running her fingers through her dreads.

"Yeah I won't be late tonight I don't think." Juliette agreed.

"Bollocks. Get some of this in you and man up." Lauren pressed a bag of cocaine into Juliette's hand. "Go on, off you go." She waved, motioning towards the restaurant.

"I'm good." Ria said. But Juliette was already heading inside. What had gotten into this girl. Sweet Juliette had turned on this trip. Ria thought she liked it at first but now she wasn't sure. By the time Juliette emerged, pupils like saucers, the girls had a table. Ria ate, Juliette and Lauren drank and drank.

"*Más señor. Más vino!*" Lauren called to the young olive skinned waiter. He blushed, and obliged, topping up their glasses as they continued various inappropriate conversations.

"Wonder how Nancy's getting on?" Ria asked.

"Well she's not messaged so she's either getting fucked or murdered." Lauren laughed at her own joke and Juliette mock hit her.

"Bloody hell Lauren don't. Do you think we should have gone with her? Maybe we should call?" Juliette said, letting her imagination run away with her.

"She'll be fine Jools. The guy owns The Hansen Galleries. He's not a murderer." Ria replied reassuringly, touching her leg under the table. She hadn't meant to but she'd done it so naturally. Juliette smiled back at her. Ria knew that look. It was time to go.

"Ladies, I'm going to leave you to have a night of drugs and wine. I'm stuffed and I'm ready for bed. Bill me in the morning." She rose, blowing them both a kiss and disappeared before they could protest.

"Bloody hell boring. No offence Juliette but that's the kind of thing you'd do, not Ria."

"Fuck off." Juliette laughed.

"No I'm serious, I've seen a different side to you this holiday and I like it! Can you come out and play more in London please?"

"Urgh I can't. I need to knuckle down when I'm back."

"Knuckle down? Sorry what?" Lauren burst into laughter. "What exactly are you knuckling down for?"

"Well you know, work. There's this promotion coming up and I really should be earning more. I mean my parents have helped me a bit with a deposit but if I want to stay in London, which I do, I need more. Urgh can we change the subject." Juliette put her head in her hands.

"I'm already getting anxiety thinking about it to be honest. This trip...I've just been able to escape it you know?"

"Yes. I do know. That's what drugs are for. To escape our boring stressful mundane lives. That and sex of course. Speaking of which. What the hell is going on with you and Nina?"

"Nothing." Juliette blushed. "We kissed, you were there."

"Pablo says you guys have been fucking? Or scissoring or whatever it is lesbians do. Does this make you a lesbian?" Lauren said pointing her cigarette at Juliette accusingly as they headed outside to smoke.

"Fucking Pablo." Juliette smiled. "Ok yes, yes we slept together. Are you happy now?"

"Exceedingly." Lauren couldn't wipe the grin off her face. "Well go on then. What was it like?"

"It was…it was good." Juliette admitted out loud for the first time.

"Did you lick her out?"

"Lauren!"

"Sorry, did you go down on her?"

"I am not discussing this." Juliette said, busying herself drinking wine and smoking continuously.

"Ok. I just want to know…was she better than a guy?"

"She was very good." Juliette said, looking Lauren straight in the eye and shutting the conversation down.

"Gosh all this talk about sex. Think I'll give Pablo a text. Nothing better than a coke fuelled fuck is there."

"Jesus." Juliette muttered, stubbing out her cigarette. "Let's go."

They headed back to the airbnb with Lauren furiously messaging Pablo to come round and fuck. Juliette wanted to message Nina but knew she shouldn't. Back at the apartment, Juliette went into her room to 'sleep' whilst Lauren waited for Pablo. In the haven of her bedroom she allowed herself to think of Nina. She loved how she dominated her. She tried to remember the taste of her pussy but it had been so long. So she thought instead of how she'd fucked her with that ice cold glass dildo. How her asshole had been hungry for that metal butt plug. She plunged her fingers inside herself. Finger fucking herself and imagining it was Nina. What she wouldn't do to feel her tongue on her clit again. One flicker would bring her to climax. She let herself moan softly as she rubbed her clit and came.

23

Nancy woke up to the smell of coffee. Henrik was already showered and dressed in a soft ecru linen shirt and pale blue levis jeans. He was barefoot and his hair was still wet.

"Last night was incredible." He smiled, sitting on the edge of the bed and handed Nancy a coffee. Nancy pulled the cover up over her bare breasts and sat up, her mane of red curls looking even more striking against the minimalist decor of the room.

"I'll just have this and go." Nancy said, sensing that Henrik had somewhere important to be.

"There's no rush. Stay as long as you like. I'm only dressed because I have meetings all day."

"You're a busy man." Nancy said as she slid out of bed and headed to the shower. Why was she being off with him. Was this her playing it cool?

"Have I upset you?" He pressed, looking confused.

"No of course not. I just better be going too. It's our last day today. We fly first thing tomorrow." She touched his arm warmly before closing the bathroom door.

It was still early, so Nancy decided to walk back to the apartment. It would take about an hour but she could do with the exercise and it would be nice to grab some breakfast on the way back. She wasn't sure how she'd left things with Henrik. There was no, *see you later* or plans to meet up when they were back in London but she did get the impression that he liked her. After Juan Felipe, she wasn't going to read too much into anything. If she never saw him again that was fine. It was simply a holiday romance.

It took longer than she thought to reach *La Rambla*. She had just ordered a smoothie from one of the street stands when she felt a tap on her shoulder. She swivelled round and practically spat out her drink. It was Juan Felipe. *Fuck. Fuck. Fuck.*

"Nancy. How are you?" He said warmly, placing his hand on her arm and smiling almost right through her.

"I'm fine." She said glaring at him and continuing to walk up *La Rambla*. He hurried after her.

"Nancy, forgive me if I've got this wrong but I'm sensing some negative energy?" He placed his hands on his temples as if experiencing a migraine.

"You'd be correct." She replied incensed. He nodded slowly with his eyes closed for a bizarre amount of time.

"I don't have time for this Juan Felipe. I liked you ok. I thought you were different. But you're not. You clearly just sleep with all your students?" She hadn't meant it to come out as a question but in doing so it revealed that she did want to know. She wanted to know if wanky dick face on reception was right.

"Nancy I am hurt by this. Are you the first student I have slept with? No. But that does not mean it is habitual. Yoga is my life. So it is not unusual for me to meet women during my practices. I do not go to bars or nightclubs. I do not use dating apps. I prefer to meet people through fate." He smiled serenely. Nancy felt herself blush with embarrassment. What he was saying made sense.

"It's just your, your colleague made out that…"

"Davide."

"Yes well Davide made out that this is what you do, just shag a different student every week."

"He said that?"

"Well no not exactly. But that's what I'm saying. He made out that I was just another shag for you." God what was she saying. She felt like a prize dick. A desperate needy dick.

"Hmm. Davide can have a cold energy. It's not the first time he has upset one of my students. For that, I can only apologise."

"Well yes it's fine." Nancy was flustered. "Look, I need to get back. I'm sorry for the misunderstanding."

"I will see you again Nancy. The universe is not finished with us." And with that he disappeared into the crowds. What on earth was going on. How was it she was more flustered over Juan Felipe than Henrik! She headed straight back to the apartment conflicted between two men she wasn't even sure were into her.

24

Back at the apartment, Ria was messaging Pieter from the beach.

"So Pieter says he can do us four tickets for 300 instead of 400. What do we think? That includes the bottomless 'brunch' and VIP loungers near the DJ set."

"I'm in." Lauren said. "It's our last day and we can't be out too late because someone booked a stupidly early flight tomorrow. So we may as well bring the night to the day."

"Yeah I'm keen." Juliette agreed as Nancy walked through the door.

"Oh here she is. The dirty stop out." Lauren clapped.

"Mature Lauren." Nancy rolled her eyes and got a glass of water.

"Tell us everything!" Lauren said.

"He was really nice. But…I bumped into Juan Felipe on my way back and to be honest I now feel like a massive dick."

"Why?" Ria asked.

"Because…for whatever reason in my fucked up head although I know on paper there is no contest between him and Henrik. I can't bloody stop thinking about Juan Felipe."

"But I thought he was an asshole? You said he was sleeping with a load of his students?" Juliette said.

"Yeah well it turns out perhaps I was a little hasty on that one. Anyway it doesn't matter because we go home tomorrow and it's highly unlikely I'll be seeing either of them again." Ria wrapped her arms around her neck.

"Fuck the both of them." She smiled. "Let's leave on a high. Pieter can get us tickets to a pool party at the W with DJ Esko today. Usually 100 a ticket but he can do four for 300. That includes the bottomless brunch and VIP loungers. You in?"

"The W? You are kidding I've literally just walked back from there. I'm in but we are taking a cab."

It didn't take long for the girls to get changed into their bikinis and coverups. They arrived at the W hotel just before midday as the pool party was well under way. The music was thumping as Norway's most famous DJ took the decks and Pieter ushered them to their loungers with sea and pool views.

"So all the alcohol is included apart from champagne. Now what can I get you?"

"Champagne please. But Pieter…we're going to need that included." Lauren winked, and put her sunglasses down.

"Ah ladies sorry no can do. I don't make the rules you know." He shrugged awkwardly but was clearly intimidated by Lauren.

"I'm sure you have a lot of influence here Pieter. You must have brought them what? At least 10,000 euros worth of business today?"

"I'll see what I can do." He said defeated, before a waitress returned with champagne on ice and four flutes.

"Don't ask don't get." Lauren exclaimed, taking great pleasure in popping it open and filling their glasses.

"Speaking of which, where's my Pablo?"

"Pablo's coming?" Juliette asked.

"Yes Nina's coming too." Lauren laughed.

"I thought this was just going to be us today?" Ria asked, sulking.

"Ria you've been a right moody cow this holiday. Are you really that pussy deprived? Are you jealous that Juliette got the only hot lesbian?" Lauren cackled.

"Fuck off Lauren." Ria bit back a bit too aggressively.

"How do you know I've not got with somebody?"

"Ermm because the only lead you've had pal is that annoying Texan."

Ria glared at Juliette. Nancy looked from Ria to Juliette.

"Leave it Lauren." Nancy said softly.

"Leave what? Be happy for our boring mate who's actually gone a little wild this holiday. You know her and Nina have fucked right? She told me last night. Said she licked pussy better than any guy."

"Lauren. What the fuck." Juliette was now fuming.

"Is that right?" Ria said, looking at Juliette. Although deep down she knew something more had happened between the two of them.

"Ria. I'm sorry."

"Why are you apologising Jools? Ria should be the one apologising for being a boring dark cloud on this trip."

"Lauren that's enough." Nancy piped up.

"I slept with Ria." Juliette said quietly. Finally confessing to Lauren.

"What?" Lauren spat out her drink. "You are kidding? What you've been sleeping with Ria and Nina? And they don't know about the other?" The gravity of Juliette's actions were suddenly apparent.

"I didn't know you'd actually been sleeping with Nina too." Nancy looked disappointed. "That was before Ria though right? Right Jools?"

"I'm really sorry." Juliette's eyes filled with tears.

"Shit there's Pablo and Nina." Lauren said stubbing out her cigarette.

"Please don't tell them about all this. Can we just forget about it?" Juliette begged.

"Forget that you fucked your best mate over? Dunno Jools, that's a hard one even for me." Lauren got up to greet Pablo and ushered him and Nina to the bar.

"Ria I'm so sorry. I don't know what's come over me this holiday. I'm not blaming the drugs but.."

"You've had countless opportunities to end things with Nina. But you've continued to see her in between me. Do you know how used that makes me feel Juliette? I really liked you."

"Ria?" Nancy was looking concerned. Suddenly this had gone from fling to feelings.

"I didn't know." Juliette said quietly.

"Oh I think you did." Ria snatched her drink up and headed to the bar.

"Nancy what shall I do?" Juliette begged in between tears.

"I honestly don't know Jools. But I think maybe you should go back to the apartment." She got up to join Ria.

Juliette grabbed her bag and ran for the exit. She wanted the world to swallow her up. She felt exhausted from the drink and the coke. Was this a come down? Or was this really how shit it felt to have all your best friends hate you. As she ran to the elevator Nina blocked the door from closing and slipped inside.

"Hey what's wrong?" She asked.

"They know about us."

"So? I thought they did anyway?"

"I've been sleeping with Ria too." Juliette bawled as she said it aloud.

"You've what?" Nina looked furious. Juliette had not anticipated this.

"I slept with her after El Bitch and then once more."

"When?" Nina demanded.

"After Samuel's party." The elevator pinged and the doors opened into the foyer. Nina followed Juliette out onto the street where she hailed a cab.

"You fucking what. After I had you at Samus you went back to that bitch?" Nina was seething.

"It's over Nina. With you. With Ria. Everything." She climbed into the taxi and Nina was left swearing to herself in Spanish.

25

Ria was on a mission. She was already two lines and a bottle of champagne down. Lauren was being a good friend for once and staying with her rather than Pablo. Nancy gazed up at the hotel. She could see the top penthouse. She wondered if Henrik was up there. Would it be weird if she went up to see?

Hey Henrik. I'm at the pool party at the W. Do you fancy joining?

Hello Nancy :) It's not really my scene but I'd love to steal you away if you want to come and see me?

Of course this wasn't his thing. He's a sophisticated Danish art gallery owner.

Give me five minutes :)

She slipped away without anyone noticing. She ruffled her hair and reapplied her lipstick in the elevator, emboldened by drink. Thank god she'd laid off the coke. She didn't get the impression that would be Henrik's scene either. As the elevator opened, Henrik was waiting for her with a grin.

"I'm so glad you messaged. I was starting to feel used." He kissed her passionately and they tumbled into the bedroom. They lay on the bed kissing and feeling each other's toned bodies. Nancy could feel his rock hard cock pushing against her leg. Henrik began unbuttoning Nancy's coverup and pulled down her bikini top to nestle his head into her breasts. Her nipples were erect and Henrik licked them slowly, working his way down her tummy before peeling her bikini bottoms off. He spun her onto all fours before bending down to lick her out from behind. She felt exposed but in a good way. She allowed herself to push her ass and pussy into his face which he seemed to love. She could feel him groaning into her as he tossed himself off. This was clearly a favourite move of his. As he came up for air he put two fingers inside her, finger fucking her hard. She wasn't usually a fan of it but it may as well have been his cock. He knew exactly which buttons to press and Nancy found herself on the brink of orgasm before he thrust himself into her, holding her ass and fucking like an athlete. His dick was so long and hard, she wanted to ride it but she was enjoying Henrik taking the lead. He bent down to kiss the nape of her neck, groaning into her ear before he filled her with cum. Nancy was desperate to relieve herself but she knew Henrik would want to finish what he started. He inserted his fingers again, expertly flicking her clit with his thumb at the same time. Nancy felt her body convulse. She was screaming so loudly she thought she was going to explode but just as she thought he was finished with her, he put his cock back in and fucked her hard till they came together.

They lay on the bed, Nancy's head in Henrik's armpit as he stroked her arm.

"How do you get so hard so quickly again?" She giggled.

"Ha, I've always had a lot of stamina I guess." He laughed shyly. "I feel very natural with you Nancy."

"Me too." She said smiling. This was the right decision. Henrik was marriage material. This could be something. Juan Felipe was a boy compared to Henrik.

26

Back at the pool party Ria was starting to get messy. Even by Lauren's standards.

"What are you looking at?" Ria slurred at Nina, as she returned.

"Fuck off Ria. Don't take what you can't handle. And I include Juliette in that." She added, sneering.

"You can have her Nina. I don't make a habit of being someone's sloppy seconds."

"Ria," Lauren whispered, "come on. Let's not do this. It's our last day."

"Byyyye." Nina said with a mock wave.

"Where have you been?" Lauren hissed as Nancy returned.

"I went to see Henrik. Is everything ok?"

"No it's not ok. Ria has had far too much coke. She's mouthing off at Nina. I haven't even been able to speak to Pablo hardly." Lauren's eyed filled with tears.

"Alright calm down. I'll stay with Ria. You go and be with Pablo." Nancy said reassuringly. "Fuck is that Madeline? Thank God Juliette's not here."

Lauren headed back over to Pablo and started kissing him but he seemed preoccupied.

"What's wrong?" Lauren cooed.

"Where's your friend? Juliette?"

"She's gone home. Why?"

"Nina is pissed man. She says she's got a video of Juliette."

"A video?"

"Yeah you know. A sex tape."

"Oh jesus." Lauren marched over to Nina and wrenched the phone from her hand. "Right where is it?"

"Give me my fucking phone back."

"Pablo says you've got a video of my friend. I want you to delete it right now. Where is it?"

"Fucking chill." Nina hissed, anxiously looking out for Madeline.

"It's not here. It's cctv from the club. But I'm going to delete it. Don't worry."

"You should have wiped it as soon as you had a chance. In fact you should have fucking turned the cameras off."

"I can't just unplug the security. Juliette knows it was running and she knows I'm going to delete it. Now fucking keep your voice down." Her expression quickly changed to a smile as she saw Madeline. "*Mi amor.*" She kissed her on the lips and held her tightly, eviling Lauren.

"I'm serious Nina." Lauren said as she walked back over to Pablo.

"Let's go back to mine babe. There's nowhere for us to sneak off here." Lauren propositioned.

"I can't, said I'd help Nina out with some business."

"What about our final fuck?" Lauren asked angrily.

"I said I'd come to London didn't I?" Pablo said, kissing her. *Great last day this was turning out to be.* The evening was coming to a natural end. It was still early but Ria seriously needed to sleep it off and Nancy was feeling bad about how things had ended with Juliette.

"Shall we call it a night?" Nancy asked Lauren, looking at Ria in a trance.

"Yeah." Lauren admitted defeat. She said goodbye to Pablo with promises they'd see each other in London and then they headed back to the airbnb.

27

The next morning, the girls sat around the table for the last time. Their taxi for the airport would be here soon but Nancy felt like she needed to play mediator beforehand.

"I think we should leave everything that happened here, here. Ok? Mistakes were made. Apologies have been made. Let's not let this ruin our friendship. You're better than this Ria."

"It's fine. I've moved on. So everyone else should too ok." Ria said defiantly, nursing the mother of all hangovers.

"I just want to say how sorry I am to all of you. Really. But especially you Ria. You didn't deserve any of this. I just hope you can forgive me in time."

"You're forgiven Jools. Honestly, I don't want to talk about this anymore. I feel like I'm on Jerry Springer. Jesus."

It didn't take long for Lauren to turn the conversation back to herself. Animatedly telling them all the plans she had for Pablo when he visited her in London.

"So we'll definitely do all the sights. He's never done them before, can you believe it? Like literally not even seen Big Ben. But how random is this right? He's been to Hull! Can you imagine?" She laughed in between mouthfuls of croissant. "His cousin studied there. So fucking random. He must think the UK is a right shit hole." No one was really listening. Nancy was in pack up mode. Ria was feeling on the cusp of throwing up and Juliette was having an identity crisis.

"Cab's here!" Nancy called. They heaved their suitcases down the four flights of stairs to the taxi. In the taxi Juliette's phone pinged.

Safe flight

It was a message from an unknown number with several images attached. Photos of her and Nina in rather compromising positions.

I'd hate for these to end up in the wrong hands.

She felt herself turn red and quickly replied back:

Who is this???

She couldn't tell the girls so she turned to the only person she could.

Nina. Someone's just sent me a load of photos from the club.

You need to delete that tape! And find out who sent these?

Juliette's phone rang. It was Nina but she couldn't answer. Not now after they'd 'made up'. She typed quickly.

I can't speak. I'm with the girls. Please can you sort this?

Nina replied instantly.

I'm on it.

Printed in Great Britain
by Amazon